Also by Ellen Hopkins
Crank
Burned

Coming soon
Glass
The sequel to *Crank*

Margaret K. McElderry Books

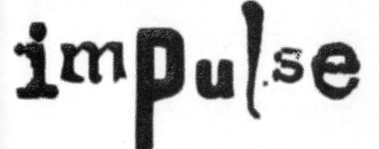

impulse

Ellen Hopkins

Margaret K. McElderry Books
New York London Toronto Sydney

Margaret K. McElderry Books
An imprint of Simon & Schuster Children's Publishing Division
1230 Avenue of the Americas, New York, New York 10020
This book is a work of fiction. Any references to historical events, real people,
or real locales are used fictitiously. Other names, characters, places, and incidents
are products of the author's imagination, and any resemblance to actual events
or locales or persons, living or dead, is entirely coincidental.
Book design by Mike Rosamilia
The text for this book is set in Janson Text.

Manufactured in the United States of America
10 9 8 7 6
Library of Congress Cataloging-in-Publication Data
Hopkins, Ellen.
Impulse / Ellen Hopkins.—1st ed.
p. cm.
Summary: Three teens who meet at Reno, Nevada's Aspen Springs mental
hospital after each has attempted suicide connect with one another in a way
they never have with their parents or anyone else in their lives.
ISBN-13: 978-1-4169-0356-7 (hardcover)
ISBN-10: 1-4169-0356-9 (hardcover)
[1. Suicide—Fiction. 2. Mental illness—Fiction.
3. Psychiatric hospitals—Fiction. 4. Interpersonal relations—Fiction.
5. Novels in verse.] I. Title.
PZ7.H7747Imp 2007
[Fic]--dc22
2006007854

This book is dedicated to my daughter, Kelly,
who helps young people like these,
and to my friend Cheryl,
who always puts others first.

Without Warning

Sometimes

you're traveling
a highway, the only road
you've ever known,
and wham! A semi
comes from nowhere
and rolls right over you.

Sometimes

you don't wake up.
But if you happen
to, you know things
will never be
the same.

Sometimes

that's not
so bad.

Sometimes

lives intersect,
no rhyme, no reason,
except, perhaps,
for a passing semi.

Triad

Three

       separate highways
       intersect at a place
       no reasonable person
       would ever want to go.

Three

       lives that would have
       been cut short, if not
       for hasty interventions
       by loved ones. Or Fate.

Three

       people, with nothing
       at all in common
       except age, proximity,
       and a wish to die.

Three

       tapestries, tattered
       at the edges and come
       unwoven to reveal
       a single mutual thread.

The Thread

Wish

    you could turn off
    the questions, turn
    off the voices,
    turn off all sound.

Yearn

    to close out
    the ugliness, close
    out the filthiness,
    close out all light.

Long

    to cast away
    yesterday, cast
    away memory,
    cast away all jeopardy.

Pray

    you could somehow stop
    the uncertainty, somehow
    stop the loathing,
    somehow stop the pain.

Act

        on your impulse,
        swallow the bottle,
        cut a little deeper,
        put the gun to your chest.

Conner

Arrival

The glass doors swing open,
in perfect sync, precisely
timed so you don't have
to think. Just stroll right in.

I doubt it's quite as easy
to turn around and walk
back outside, retreat to
unstable ground. Home turf.

An orderly escorts me down
spit-shined corridors, past
tinted Plexiglas and closed,
unmarked doors. Mysteries.

One foot in front of the other,
counting tiles on the floor so
I don't have to focus the blur
of painted smiles, fake faces.

A mannequin in a tight blue
suit, with a too-short skirt
(and legs that can wear it),
in a Betty Boop voice halts us.

I'm Dr. Boston. Welcome to
Aspen Springs. I'll give you
the tour. Paul, please take his
things to the Redwood Room.

Aspen Springs. Redwood Room.
As if this place were a five-star
resort, instead of a lockdown
where crazies pace. Waiting.

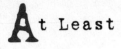

At Least

It doesn't have a hospital
stink. Oh yes, it's all very
clean, from cafeteria chairs
to the bathroom sink. Spotless.

But the clean comes minus
the gag-me smell, steeping
every inch of that antiseptic
hell where they excised

the damnable bullet. I
wonder what Dad said when
he heard I tried to put myself
six feet under—and failed.

I should have put the gun
to my head, worried less
about brain damage, more
about getting dead. Finis.

Instead, I decided a shot
through the heart would
make it stop beating, rip
it apart to bleed me out.

I couldn't even do that
right. The bullet hit bone,
left my heart in one piece.
In hindsight, luck wasn't

with me that day. Mom
found me too soon, or my
pitiful life might have ebbed
to the ground in arterial flow.

I thought she might die too,
at the sight of so much blood
and the thought of it staining
her white Armani blouse.

> *Conner, what have you done?*
> she said. *Tell me this was just*
> *an accident.* She never heard
> my reply, never shed a tear.

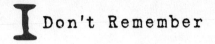Don't Remember

Much after that, except
for speed. Ghostly red lights,
spinning faster and faster,
as I began to recede from

consciousness. Floating
through the ER doors,
frenzied motion. A needle's
sting. But I do remember,

just before the black hole
swallowed me, seeing Mom's
face. Her furious eyes
followed me down into sleep.

It's a curious place, the
Land of Blood Loss and
Anesthesia, floating through it
like swimming in sand. Taxing.

After a while, you think you
should reach for the shimmering
surface. You can't hold your
breath, and even if you could,

it's dark and deep and bitter
cold, where nightmares and truth
collide, and you wonder if death
could unfold fear so real. Palpable.

So you grope your way up into
the light, to find you can't
move, with your arms strapped
tight and overflowing tubes.

And everything hits you like
a train at full speed. Voices.
Strange faces. A witches' stewpot
of smells. Pain. Most of all,

pain.

Tony

Just Saw

A new guy check in. Tall,
        built, with a way fine face,
and acting too tough to tumble.
        He's a nutshell asking to crack.
Wonder if he's ever let a guy
        touch that pumped-up bod.

They gave him the Redwood
        Room. It's right across
from mine—the Pacific
        Room. Pretty peaceful in
here most of the time, long
        as my meds are on time.

Ha. Get it? Most of the time,
        if my meds are on time. If you
don't get it, you've never
        been in a place like this,
never hung tough from one
        med call till the next.

Wasted. That's the only way
        to get by in this "treatment
center." Nice name for a loony
        bin. Everyone in here is crazy
one way or another. Everyone.
        Even the so-called doctors.

Most of 'em are druggies.
        Fucking loser meth freaks.
I mean, if you're gonna
        purposely lose your mind,
you want to get it back some
        day. Don't you? Okay, maybe not.

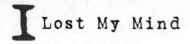Lost My Mind

A long time ago, but it
            wasn't exactly my idea.
Shit happens, as they say,
            and my shit literally hit
the fan. But enough sappy
            crap. We were talking drugs.

I won't tell you I never tried
            crystal, but it really wasn't
my thing. I saw enough
            people, all wound up, drop
over the edge, that I guess
            I decided not to take that leap.

I always preferred creeping
            into a giant, deep hole where
no bad feelings could follow.
            At least till I had to come up
for air. I diddled with pot first, but
            that tasty green weed couldn't drag

me low enough. Which mostly
          left downers, "borrowed" from
medicine cabinets and kitchen
          cabinets and nightstands.
Wherever I could find them.
          And once in a while—not often,

because it was pricey and tough
          to score—once in a while, I
tumbled way low, took a ride
          on the H train. Oh yeah,
that's what I'm talking about.
          A hot shot clear to hell.

I Wasn't Worried

About getting hooked, though
        I knew plenty of heroin addicts.
I didn't do it enough, for one
        thing. Anyway, I figured
I'd be graveyard rot before
        my eighteenth birthday.

It hasn't quite worked out
        that way, though I've got
a few months to go. And
        once I get out of here, I'll
have a better shot at it. Maybe
        next time I won't try pills.

I mean, you'd think half a bottle
        of Valium would do the trick.
Maybe it would have, but I had
        to toss in a fifth of Jack Daniels.
Passed out, just as I would
        have expected. What I didn't

expect was waking up, head stuck
        to the sidewalk, mired in puke.
Oh yeah, I heaved the whole
        fucking mess. Better yet, guess
who happened by? You got it.
        One of the city's finest.

Poor cop didn't know what
        to do—clean me up, haul
me in, or puke himself. So
        he did all three, only dispatch
said to take me to the ER.
        Hospital first. Loony bin

later.

Vanessa

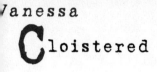loistered

I can't remember
when it has snowed
so much, yards
and yards of lacy ribbons,
wrapping the world in white.
Was it three years ago? Ten?

Memory is a tenuous thing,
like a rainbow's end
or a camera with a failing lens.
Sometimes my focus
is sharp, every detail
clear as the splashes
of ice, fringing the eaves;
other times it is a hazy
field of frost, like the meadow
outside my window.
I think it might be a meadow.
A lawn? A parking lot?

Is it even a window
I'm looking through,
or only cloudy panes
of vision, opening
on drifts of ivory
linens—soft cotton,
crisp percale—
my snow just
a blizzard of white
noise?

I Hate This Feeling

Like I'm here, but I'm not.
Like someone cares.
But they don't.
Like I belong somewhere
else, anywhere but here,
and escape lies just past
that snowy window,
cool and crisp as the February
air. I consider the streets
beyond, bleak as the bleached
bones of wilderness
scaffolding my heart.
Just a stone's throw away.

But *she's* out there,
stalking me, haunting me.
I know she can't get me
in here. Besides, I'm too
tired to pick myself up
and make a break for it.
So I just sit here, brain
wobbling. Tipping.
Tripping on Prozac.

I wonder if they give
everyone Prozac on their twice-
daily med deliveries.
Do they actually try to
diagnose first, or do they
think everyone is depressed,
just by virtue of being here?

My arm throbs
and I look at the bandage,
a small red stain
beginning to slither.
Did I pop a stitch?
Wouldn't that be luscious?

The First Cut

Wasn't the deepest.
No, not at all.
It was like the others,
a subtle rend of anxious skin,
a gentle pulse of crimson,
just enough to hush the demons
shrieking inside my brain.
But this time they wouldn't
shut up. Just kept on
howling, like Mama,
when she was in a bad way.

Worst thing was, the older
I got, the more I began to see
how much I resembled Mama,
falling in and out of the blue,
then lifting up into the white.
That day I actually
thought about howling.
So I gave myself to the knife,
asked it to bite a little
harder, chew a little deeper.
The hot, scarlet rush
felt so delicious
I couldn't stop there.

The blade might have reached
bone, but my little
brother, Bryan,
barged into the bathroom,
found me leaning against
Grandma's new porcelain
tub, turning its unstained
white pink.
You should
have heard

him scream.

Pain Isn't the Worst Thing

At least you know you're not
just a shadow, darkening
someone's wall, a silhouette
thrust haphazardly into their lives.

My fingers trace the sunken
scar as I pace the plain room,
counting steps from near wall
to far, right to left. Eight by ten.

Eighty square feet to call my
own for the next how many
days? Eighty square feet, with no
television or phone, only two

tiny beds, a closet, and one
vinyl chair near the window—
a window that doesn't open,
not even a crack for air.

Two beds. Does that mean I
might get a roommate soon?
Some paranoid schizo, rambling
on through the suffocating night?

Well, hey. Maybe he'd think
that he was the one who drew
the short straw, having to share
a room with some totally

whacked-out freak. I wonder
how long it would take him
to realize I'm right as sin— it's
the rest of the world that's wrong.

I'm not even sure how I
qualify for admission to
Aspen Springs. Does wanting
to die equal losing your mind?

It Doesn't Seem

So incredibly insane to me.
In fact, it seems courageous
to, for once in your life, make
others react to a plan you set

in motion. Not that I meant
to cause anyone pain, only
to make them realize that
everyone has flaws. Even me.

Especially me. Hell, I'm
so flawed I wound up here,
with sixty defective humans.
Odd, to think I made the A-list.

I open the dresser drawers,
start to put away my neatly
folded clothes. No Sears. No
Wal-Mart, but Macy's. Nordstrom's.

I can see my mom, stalking
aisle after aisle of designer
jeans, intent on the latest
style, perfect eye-catching fit.

I hear her tell the silicone
saleslady, *Nothing for me
today. I'm shopping for my
son. He fails to comprehend*

*fashion. If it wasn't for me,
I swear he'd choose nothing
but T-shirts and khaki. Now
where will I find the Calvin Klein?*

I Reach

For a lavender Ralph Lauren
shirt, ironed into submission,
collar starched into crisp, straight
Vs, no hint of dirt or sweat.

Back at school, clothes like this
made me the cream of my senior
class, at least in the eyes of
twisted dream girls and cheerleaders.

Oh yes, Mom's expensive tastes
went a long way toward getting
me laid. Did she have a clue
that all those dollars spent on

haute couture allowed her sweet
young son to feed his appetite
for carnal pleasure—to divvy
himself among a stable of fillies?

As the vile green walls defy
my stare, some evil makes me
wad Lauren shirt and Jockey
underwear into a wrinkled lump.

Okay, maybe that's a little
crazy. Maybe I belong here,
after all. Maybe crazy is
preferable to staying strong

when you just want to break down
and weep. But big boys don't cry.
Do they? So instead I'll just
keep jamming clothes into drawers,

grinning.

Tony
When You Try

The big S, the first thing
            they do is lock you away
by yourself, like you
            might try to do someone
else in, 'cause you didn't
            do yourself good enough.

Then some lame nurse's aide
            checks in on you every
fifteen minutes, probably
            hoping you've found a way
to finish yourself off and save
            them a whole lot of trouble.

After a couple of days
            the main person you want
to strangle is the annoying
            dude who keeps poking his
head through your door.
            How ya doing? Okay?

So by the time you finally
        get to see your shrink,
you're irritated to begin
        with. And she asks you
to tell her how you feel
        and all you can think

to answer is "pissed."
        Then she wants to know
just whom you're angry with
        and you decide maybe you
shouldn't tell her the friggin'
        nurse's aide, in case they worry

you might try to strangle
        him. So you try to think
of someone else you're
        mad at, and the unavoidable
answer pops into your
        warped little brain: everyone.

They Kept Me

Locked up in isolation
       for almost two weeks.
See, you have to make
       Level One to go to school
and eat with everyone else.
       You arrive here at Level Zero.

Nothing. That's exactly what
       you are until you can
prove to them that you
       won't save up your meds
and OD or lynch yourself
       with strips of your sheets.

So you hang out in your room,
       maybe reading a book
(approved literature) or
       journaling with a felt pen.
No pencils (no leads).
       No pens (no points).

Maybe I could think up a way
          to kill yourself with a felt pen.
Maybe I could sell the idea
          to the dozen or so freaks
in here determined to do
          themselves in. Maybe I'll use

it myself. Am I saying that
          I'm a freak? Effing A!
I quit worrying about it
          a long time ago. Better
a freak than a total loser.
          Better a freak than a liar.

So far, everyone I've
          ever met has been a liar.
Everyone but Phillip,
          my only true friend, my
savior. Never hurt me, never
          coerced me. Never lied to me.

The Worst Liars

Are the ones everyone thinks
       would never, ever tell a lie.
The teachers who act like
       they care about you, then
turn you in for smoking a cig
       or kissing someone in the hall.

Or the plain Jane, churchgoing
       soccer moms who plaster on
some anonymous face, then
       sneak out once a week or so,
pretending they're off with
       girlfriends when they're really

looking for ways to get laid.
       No, my ma wasn't one of
those. She made no bones
       about getting laid, something
she did plenty of. Laid by no-
       good, nasty losers, single,

married, it didn't matter,
        long as they had a few bucks
and the necessary attachments,
        in good working order. Beat
up. Knocked up. Messed up.
        She got all of those things,

didn't care. Worse, she
        didn't give two cents
about what her "lifestyle"
        did to me. Her son.
Her only son, because
        after one particularly

ugly abortion, her body
        decided it had had enough
of Ma's mistreatment and
        formed scar tissue around
her ovaries. The odds of my
        having a sibling shrank

to nil.

Vanessa

I Heard My Brother's Scream

Through the cloud
that had veiled my brain,
coloring everything crimson.
It seemed to last forever,
that scream. Poor Bryan.
He's only eight,
too little to understand
that dying isn't something
to fear. It's a comfort.

I felt comfortable, dying
that afternoon, and would
have, except Grandma
happens to be a nurse—
a good nurse, hard,
wise, through and through.
And she happened to be home.
She calmly dialed 911,
wrapped my arm
in a soft yellow towel
which looked ochre through
the scarlet mist.

Stay with me, Vanessa,
she repeated over and over.

I remember that,
and I remember one EMT,
with blondish hair and a killer mouth
that refused to say a word,
except to his partner.
I remember his eyes the most—
brilliant blue, and filled
with disgust.

> Grandma rode in the ambulance
> with me, and the last thing
> I remember is telling her I was sorry
> for staining her new bathtub.
> *Screw the tub, Vanessa,*
> *there's help for that.*
> *And there's help for you.*

Which Is How I Wound Up Here

Left hand stitched neatly
back in place.
They tell me it will
be good as new, but my fingers
feel like they belong
to someone else and don't
want to be attached to me.
Nothing does.

I've been here about a week,
I think, watching it snow
and listening through the walls
to other girls, sicker than I am.
They talk about themselves,
about the things they've done,
the things they'd like to do.
Parents. Teachers. Counselors.
So-called friends.
They'd all better run when
those sociopaths find their way
back outside.

There are boys here too,
somewhere. I know because
sometimes I hear the girls
call to them down the hall.

The things they say!
A truck driver would blush.
I would never talk that way
to Trevor. He walks on water.
I want him to think I do too.
For a while, he did, or at least
he pretended to.

I did things with Trevor
I wouldn't dare confess
to anyone—things I didn't
know anyone did.
But he wanted me to,
so I did. That's what you do
when you love someone,
right?

The Door Opens

Death watch crew, come
to check up on me.
They've been after me
all week, first every
fifteen or twenty minutes,
then every hour or two,
making sure I don't rip
stitches and let my hand
drop off after all.

> *Hello, Vanessa*, says Paul,
> who is fabulously tall
> and almost as wide
> as the door. He hands me
> my morning pill, unwraps
> my bandage, peeks underneath.
> *Dr. Boston says if you join us*
> *for group this afternoon, she'll*
> *award you Level One. You*
> *could start school tomorrow.*

So far I've avoided group,
preferring to semi-vent
my pent-up insanity in private

therapy sessions—Vanessa
Angela O'Reilly, closed book.
But I have to admit I'm
tired of this room, weary
of these auburn walls.
Maybe, if I stash my meds,
I can keep my mouth
shut and just listen to the sob
stories, passed around
the big circle like joints.
Maybe I'll find them entertaining.
So I tuck the Prozac
under my tongue, nod.

"Okay."

Conner
Suitcase Emptied

I walk to the sealed window,
stare at the glistening world
outside. Buried in snow.
Glare threatens my eyes

but I don't turn away. I like it.
Up the hall come deliberate
footsteps. Suddenly they
stall and the door creaks open.

> It's Paul, the rather large
> guy who escorted me here.
> *Everything good?* It's almost
> a sigh. *All settled in?*

"Uh-huh." I offer a (not)
genuine smile. "Unpacked
and ready to party. When
does the shindig begin?"

> Paul, who is not amused,
> tosses a pair of gray sweats
> on the bed. *Put these on.*
> He crosses the room, opens

drawers, assesses sundries
and wrinkled clothes as I slip
into the sweats. *You'll wear
those except for Sunday services*

*or when your parents visit.
Now Dr. Starr would like
to chat. Please come with me.*
He draws to the far side

of the door, allows me by,
takes his place at my elbow,
reminding me I no longer
own the space around me.

Dr. Starr Isn't Like Dr. Boston

No tight navy suit, no
miniscule skirt. Nothing
about her hints nymph
or flirt. She's a bulldog.

She motions for me to
take a chair, studies me
as I move, as if the very
way I plant myself there

can tell her something
of import. She stays silent
for several long seconds.
Finally, as if holding court,

she lifts her chin, sights
down her nose, and asks,
Why are you here, Conner?
An unsettling energy flows

through the room, and it
emanates from the canine
Dr. Starr. Her patronizing
tone activates my inner

mute button. I answer with
a small shrug, and she gives
me a grin worthy of Hannibal
Lecter—evil, overtly smug.

> *You don't know? Don't you*
> *think it's time to find out?*
> The "f" elicits a saliva spray.
> The bulldog doesn't even blink.

> *I realize you don't want to*
> *be here. But until you give*
> *me a hint about just what*
> *you fear, you can't get better.*

Her voice is almost gentle,
and part of me wants to
give her what she wants.
The smart part says no way.

Play the Game

I instruct myself, give her
a little taste of what
she wants to hear. After
all, we don't want to waste

a perfectly good shrink
session. So I settle deep
into my chair, search for
some vapid confession.

Finding none I wish
to give voice to, I decide Dr.
Bulldog has given me
no other choice but to lie.

"It was really all a huge
mistake. I was goofing
around and the gun just
went off, for God's sake.

I mean, you'd think my
dad would have left
the safety on." I almost
feel bad for blaming him.

But her eyes tell me she's
heard the line before. With
quiet ferocity, she says,
Not another word, Conner.

You believe this is a game,
and you may be right.
But if you think you can
play it better than me, think

again.

Tony

I'm Glad I'm an Only Child

Ma didn't deserve kids.
        I mean, if it had been up
to her—impossible, all
        things considered—I'd be
back on the streets right now.
        Or maybe I'd have already

finished myself off. No, it
        wasn't dear old Ma who
paid my way to Aspen
        Springs. According to Dr. B,
it was, in fact, dear old dad.
        Dad, who dumped Ma and me

when I was still shitting
        green. 'Course, looking
back, I guess he had every
        reason to leave Ma in
his dust. But did he ever
        once think about me?

Anthony Ceccarelli III.
        Medium height. Medium
build. Medium brown
        hair. A medium chip off
the ol' block. Where was
        medium Dad all that time?

Dr. B says he lives at Tahoe,
        has his own insurance office,
makes decent dough. Ma
        never left Reno, except
when she was working out
        at "the ranch" near Dayton.

Ranching hookers. They
        do that in parts of Nevada.
Funny, if it wasn't so sick.
        Did Dad know? And what
made him decide he gives
        a damn about me now?

The Clock Reminds Me

It's time for group. I open
     my door, nudge my hand into
          the hall. A faceless voice
               shouts, *What's up, Ceccarelli?*
"May I go to group, sir?"
     Stay polite. Earn ten points.

          You may. Don't get lost
             along the way, though.
     Old joke, not funny.
     Still, I chortle and say,
"I'll do my best, sir.
     You know how confusing

these halls can be, though."
     Yeah. Follow the yellow
line to the classrooms,
     white to the dining hall.
The blue one leads to
     the conference rooms.

Mommy Long Legs waits,
        black widow–style, in
room C-3. Most guys
        would call her a fox,
I guess. But to me she's
        all spider, poison stashed

in hidden fangs. Yes, Dr.
        Boston's questions sink
clear through flesh, into
        bone. She's after marrow,
but she hasn't managed
        to get much of mine yet.

Funny thing. No one but
        me seems to recognize
how her Barbie-doll act
        covers up a real lack
of charm. She's a user.
        Same as everyone here.

We Gather

In room C (for Conference)-3,
          six crazies, looking to
unload. Or thinking of ways
          to avoid it. There's Schizo
Stanley, three hundred pounds
          of loaded gun, who tried to off

his little brother. Yeah,
          he denies it, but hmm . . .
wonder how Daddy's Xanax
          got mixed into Junior's milk.
On the far side of the table
          sits Lowball Lori, princess

of depression. I bet at
          home she wore nothing
but black—clothes,
          makeup, mood. Next to her
is Do-Me Dahlia, who
          uses sex like most people

use money. I heard she
       tried to put the moves
on Dr. Starr, even. Yech!
       What an ugly picture!
Jesus-save-me Justin
       lurks in one corner,

greasy hair hanging in
       his eyes, while Toot-
it-all Todd rocks back
       and forth, as if his past
pursuits haven't quite
       deserted his system.

Just as Dr. Boston says
       it's time to start, the door
opens. Someone new steps
       inside. She's pretty (did *I* think
that?), with copper hair and
       startling eyes, and her name's

Vanessa.

Vanessa
Seven Pairs of Eyes

Pierce me as I walk into the room.
I already know I can't
measure up to Dr. Boston's
expectations—she'll want
me to open my head and let
this crowd of eyes peer
into my psyche.
I want to turn and run.

> *Please sit down, Vanessa,*
> urges Dr. Boston.
> *We're ready to start.*

If I can't run, I want to
scream. I want to scream,
but I can't find my voice,
hidden somewhere
in the indigo sea that has
swamped my brain.
Blue. Blue. Deep, dark blue.
The blue that fills me with desire,
the desire to find a small,
sharp blade and watch
blood run, red.

Vanessa? Dr. Boston's
voice swims down through
the blue, disturbs me enough
to set my feet in motion.

The eyes follow me as I sit
beside the guy with the most
startling eyes of all—
round, dark eyes, with
gold flecks. Eyes that look
like they've glimpsed
behind the gates of hell.

So Why Are His Eyes

The only ones mine want to meet?
I can feel the girls, taking
measure, and part of me
wants to turn and offer my own
assessment. The bigger
part is consumed by blue.

> *Hey, Vanessa, I'm Tony,*
> says the guy with hellfire
> eyes. I would have expected
> a deeper voice from someone
> who has shaken hands
> with the devil.

And why do I think that?
He seems friendly enough. In fact,
he's the only one in the room
who bothers with introductions.
The others sit, staring,
in impassioned silence.
Tony glances around the room.

What's up, people?
Usually you won't shut up.
Now you've got nothing to say
just because a pretty girl
walks through the door?

Well, that woke them up!
Everyone looks simply
stunned, including Dr. Boston.
Is it because I'm anything
but pretty? Or a less likely reason?

> The guy with dishrag
> hair finally opens
> his mouth. *I thought you*
> *only thought dudes were*
> *pretty, Ceccarelli.*

The room explodes
with laughter. I guess
the session has officially begun.

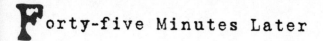

Forty-five Minutes Later

I know a lot more about most
of the people in C-3.
Tony is pretty cool, for a gay
guy who tried to commit suicide.
He didn't really talk about why,
only said that it's not easy
being queer and living on the street.
"Queer." His word. To me
it means strange, but he doesn't
seem near as strange as Justin,
who expects Armageddon any second,
or Todd, who lost a few too
many brain cells to crystal meth,

or Stanley, who's a total lunatic.
I mean, he spoke at length
about torturing insects—
I tattered their wings and tore
off their legs, joint by joint,
watched them crawl
in circles, like little lost
infants, until they decided to die.

Somehow, I doubt bugs
were his only victims.
Dahlia hasn't said one word,
just sits there with her nose
in the air. Every once in awhile,
she licks her lips, like a lioness
lording it over prey.

> Finally, Lori begins to talk
> about the pain that forces
> her down into a figurative
> grave—deep, damp, just her size.
> *It's hard to climb out sometimes.*

I try to look inside her
head, see if the color in
there is navy blue, like
the space I'm treading

now.

Conner

Brain Poked and Prodded

But still holding secrets,
I glance over at Dr. Starr,
who's locked in a computer
screen trance, typing words—

my thoughts, her analysis—
at a steady thirty-per-
minute pace. I tingle,
heady with a synthesis

of emotions. I feel
satisfied, that I didn't break
down, didn't confess major
sin, open my mouth too wide.

I feel lonely, displaced, yet
secure within the silence
curtaining each cubicle.
This is a detour, that's all.

I feel relieved to have to
admit a little of what's
inside my head. Sometimes
I think it might split wide,

cracked by the upheaval
bubbling beneath my skull.
But most people think there's
nothing troubling me at all.

At least they didn't used to.
Who knows what they think
of me now, which way the wind
of small-town gossip blows.

Finally Dr. Starr looks up.
We've got a lot of work to do,
Conner. A lot of work, indeed.
But not today. You may go.

Dismissed by the Bulldog

Stephanie guides my way
along the blue line. She
could pass for a Stephan, tall,
broad, and strong, but her eyes

tell a different story.
I discern a softness there,
compassion I want to wade
into. We turn a corner

and the blue line merges
with a thread of yellow,
another of white. I wonder
where all the crazies have fled,

and just then I hear voices,
leaking out of the rec room.
Two are shouting, one merely
speaking, trying to keep

a handle on the unfolding
situation—from what I
can tell, the probable
annihilation of one

of the dueling duo. Stephanie
shifts into takedown mode.
Wait right here, she commands.
It's a mistake to leave me

alone, and we both know it.
I choose not to play the wild
card she's dealt me. One day
I'll use it to my advantage.

A woman like that will work
like clay—soften her up, touch
her just right, the sculptor
is guaranteed to have his way.

Back in My Room

Walled in by this impossibly
ugly shade of green, I wait for
my evening meal, no doubt
delayed by the incident

in the rec room. Will I
ever get used to living
with paranoid mutants who
endeavor to win games

of pool by swallowing
the chalk? Between that, no
food, and Dr. S wanting me
to talk, all in all, it's been a

miserable day, almost
as rotten as those leading
up to that one, the one
best left forgotten unless

I want to drop down again
into a pit of despair. God
knows I've spent much too
much time floundering there.

I suppose I could have
shared that information
with dear Dr. Bulldog.
But no, I spared us both

a sordid tale of Conner
the incompetent. Hard
to believe that perfect me
underwent such complete

demolition in the space
of four short months. First-
string to benchwarmer, grades
through the floor, and all because

of her.

Tony

I Keep Watching

Pretty Vanessa as the group
            tries to freak her out, whether
that's spilling spine-chilling
            tales or clamming up altogether.
Nothing really fazes her,
            except maybe Stanley's bullshit.

The longer we sit here,
            the further she withdraws,
like a turtle holing up
            in its shell, expecting
a major rollover. I want
            to reach under and yank her

back out again. "How
            about you, Vanessa?" I ask.
"What brings you to our
            home away from home?
Are you really fucked-up or
            just totally misunderstood?"

Everyone laughs. It's an
            inside joke, one we're all
privy to, except Vanessa,
            whose brown velvet
eyes stay hitched to the
            tabletop. Not good enough.

"'Cause personally, I'm both
            fucked-up *and* misunderstood.
Can't somebody *get* me,
            please?" This time, even
the Black Widow laughs.
            Finally Vanessa lifts her eyes

and she gifts us with a smile.
            Then she shows us the arm
she's been hiding, the one
                              wrapped in white like a
                        ball-game hot dog. She smiles.
                              I guess this is why I'm here.

One Cut or More?

That's the first thought
            to grab hold of my brain
and give it a rattle. Was
            this charming little thing
into self-mutilation, or
            shopping for a coffin?

Before I can open my
            mouth to ask, Stanley
slobbers, *Hey, cool.*
            Tell us about the blood.
Did it make a big puddle?
            Did it spurt or just dribble?

                        Dr. Boston clears her throat.
                                    I think we're finished for today.
                        Odd. You'd think she'd want
            to jump all over that bit
of psychology. Then I notice
            her face has drained, white.

Hmmm. Something about
        blood? Have to file that
away for another day.
        Good ol' Stanley has caused
quite the commotion.
                    And now, as he walks out
                the door, he adds, *I still want*
                        to hear about the blood.

Which makes Todd grin
        and Justin start praying.
Lori and Dahlia lean their
        heads together and whisper.

Vanessa falls to the back
        of the pack, and though
I know I should have no
        contact, I touch her arm.
"I'm sorry," I say. And she

                    turns. *It's okay. Not your fault.*

The Grim Reapers

Appear in the hall. Dr.
       Boston must have buzzed
them, afraid of—of what?
       We're all behaving
quite peaceably, though
       a part of me would like

to rip Stanley to pieces.
       Join the club, he'd tell me.
Paul and Stephanie divide
       us according to gender
and herd us up the hall.
       At the far end, the girls

turn left and we go right,
       with me bringing up
the rear of the pack.
                    Move it, Ceccarelli, urges
               Paul. *You walk like an
                 old woman.* . . . His unfinished

thought hangs in the air:
>*or maybe a young woman.*

I wonder if I'm his
>kind of woman. . . . Never

know about these big
>mooks. "Gym-dandies,"

I call 'em. Before he got
>sick, Phillip was a big

guy, at least that's what
>he told me. And I believed

him. Phillip was the one
>person who never lied to me.

I glance back over my
>shoulder at Vanessa's

retreating behind. Damn,
>she's something special.

But why do I think so?
>Why would I care in

the least?

Vanessa

Brain Swimming

In swirls of blue, I follow
the other girls up the corridor.
I feel eyes on my back
and turn to find Tony,
staring at me. He waves
and I half-wave back, unsure
of his motivation.
Can't be lust. Friendship?
Daddy would die
if he thought
I'd made friends
with a gay guy.

> Once he told me,
> *God had a plan,*
> *and it didn't include*
> *wangs in bung holes.*

Gross, I know, but it's
how they talk in the military,
just another way of cutting
themselves off from the truth
of what they do.
Not that I'm complaining.

It's tough, being
a hostile presence
in a more hostile land,
he said one time.
You do what ya gotta
do to stay alive. And
you trust your instinct.

Aspen Springs is a hostile
land, the people here crazier
than most soldiers
I know. And at the moment,
my instincts are shouting
to do what I gotta do
just to get by.

Drowning in Blue

Pulled deeper and deeper
into the void,
I dig down
into my pocket,
find the capsule I stashed,
first beneath a flap of tongue,
then in a cave of fleece.
I hold it like a jewel,
the key to some magic
kingdom where only good
feelings are allowed.

Funny, but sometimes all I feel
is good. More than good.
Great. Invincible.
When Mama felt like that,
Daddy called her manic.
But why is mania bad,
if it means you're on top
of the world, where
everything is white? Bright.

I wish I were up there now,
instead of treading water
in this damn blue hole.
This magic pill won't fly
me there. It will only take
me halfway, to what others
call normal and I call gray—
toeing a straight gray line
is all medication is good for.
Bad genes have doomed me
to seesaw, white to blue
and back again,
for the rest of my pitiful life.

And the thought of that
makes me want
to open a vein,
experience pain,
know I'm alive, despite
this living death.

I Swallow the Capsule

Wait for the flood of silver
to gush through my bloodstream,
settle in my brain.
Outside, darkness comes
to rest upon the snow, shadows
the ordinary world.
Why can't I live, ordinary?

Which brings me back to my mother,
who gifted me with this odd
disorder—up, down, right, left,
never a straight line, until
I got here, to this house of control,
where they believe they can
tell you how to think,
how to manage the feelings
that never quite go away.
The funny thing is, they still
haven't diagnosed
my manic-depressive playground.

Oh yes, I know all about
the disorder. It's everywhere
on the Internet—clinical
studies, message boards,
bipolar chat rooms.
Yet these so-called health-
care professionals can't
see past the cutting,
to the highs and lows
that invite such release.

I guess I'm supposed
to tell them—isn't that
what therapy's all about?
But it's a lot more fun
watching them flounder
about, halfway trying
to earn their annual

60K.

Conner

I Haven't Let Myself

Think about her since this
whole stinking mess began.
Emily. The name suggests
she has a soul, but where

she hides it is a complete
mystery. I can't believe
I fell so hard for someone
with a heart of lead. Emily.

Her smile is like summer
moonlight—beautiful
and magical, with a fire
that could melt the night.

I flop on the bed, close my
eyes, try to conjure her
beside me—the scent of her
skin, the silk of her thighs,

the breathless melody
of her voice. I would be
with her now, if she had
allowed me that choice.

But no, she had to worry,
not about right or wrong,
but about how people
might talk. *What would they say,*

she asked, more than once, *if
they knew?* I wasn't sure
exactly who "they" were,
but it was certainly true

that nasty tongues would gossip.
At stake were both our worlds.
I didn't care, but it was
a risk she wouldn't take.

Now That I've Opened

That bottle of memories,
they're pouring out like wine,
crimson and bittersweet.
Ignoring the throbbing pain,

I think back to a crisp fall
Saturday morning, my parents
and sister hundreds of miles
away in California.

Cara is my twin, though
we're about as alike as
snowflakes—a general
resemblance, but peer under

a microscope, and we're
completely different. Cara's
in-your-face, while I handle
things much more discreetly.

You might call me sneaky,
though I'd call me clever,
and on that particular
day, all by myself, clever

me was in need of company.
Emily and I had not
yet been together, but
she was most definitely

on my radar. She was
far above the usual
objects of my lust—sleek
and bronzed, fearless of the star

raining radiation on
this ozone-deprived planet.
The only thing she ever
feared was our short-lived love.

I Knew None of That Then

I only knew she was the
prettiest thing ever to run
by our house. She was a falcon
on the wing, and I wanted

to fly along. She jogged
past every morning, around
eight. That day I stood like
a fisherman waiting to cast

his line and reel in something
worth trawling for. I watched
her sinewy body run by
before calling out her name.

"Emily." She turned and gave
a probing look, as if she'd
never seen me before. And
here I'd been disrobing her

regularly in my over-
active imagination.
I guess she was lonely too.
Unseemly fascination

made her do an about-face.
Panting gently, she drew even.
Hello, Conner. How can I
help you this enchanting day?

Several things came quickly
to mind, things to save for later.
My eyes poked hers. "I just wanted
you to know I find you quite

beautiful."

Tony
Dinner's a Little Late Tonight

Guess there was some kind
        of problem in the rec room.
Figures it would be a night
        when I could chow down
a horse. Okay, maybe not
        a horse. But half a cow.

Food's a funny thing.
        When I was a little kid,
we never had much food,
        but I don't remember
being hungry. Wonder
        how Ma managed to feed

me when I was an actual
        baby. Formula, I hear, costs
major bucks, and I just
        can't see her letting me
snuggle up against her
        titties. Those things

were bait, and not for
        babies. No sir, I can't
imagine how I made
        it past the mewling stage.
I feel like mewling now.
        At least here, they can't

slap you around to shut
        you up. Not that they
don't ever touch you
        at all. Takedowns.
Cavity searches after
        visits from home.

Once in a while, when
        someone "in charge"
is in a bad mood, you
        might even catch a "playful"
kick in the seat, or a teeth-
        rattling shoulder shake.

But Bloody Cuts and Bruises

Are not something you're
            going to see here. No sir.
Except maybe for Vanessa's.
            And why is she in my thoughts
again? I have to admit I'd like
            to peek beneath that bandage.

I'll probably see her at dinner
            tonight, not that they let
the guys and the girls sit
            anywhere close to each
other. I guess they think
            crappy food is an aphrodisiac.

A time or two or three,
            I have seen some serious
make-out sessions—
            male/female, male/male,
female/female. Love.
            Lust. The need to feel close.

The need to feel safe
        because someone dares
to wrap their arms around
        you in this cold, sterile place.
The need to feel. I even
        half-believe the story

about Dahlia and Dr. Starr.
        What better way to grab
preferential treatment?

                        Oh my lovely, deep-creased
                psychologist, let me stick
                        my tongue down your throat.

Nothing new for Dahlia.
        Would be nothing new
for me, either. What's
        new is that I haven't
strayed down that path
        since I've been here.

Mostly Because

For once in my life, I
        don't have to have sex.
No one demands it in
        exchange for drugs,
ten minutes of disgust
        for a well-deserved rush.

No one expects it in
        exchange for food,
just a burger and fries,
        please; for a hot shower
to wash off the streets,
        a warm bed to crash in.

Most of all, no one is
        forcing me to. I try
not to look back on
        the moment when
my pitiful life turned
        unbearable. Unthinkable.

Try to blot it out, scrub
        it out, rip it out of my
brain completely.
        But you can't forget
something like that,
        no matter how much you

drink, snort, or shoot into
        your veins. The memory
stalks you forever and
        creeps up to maul you
like a rabid dog, when
        you least expect it.

Like now.

Vanessa

Thank God

The intercom squawks.
Okay, Happy Campers,
dinner is served.

Happy Campers?
Must I join that sorority?
Doesn't much matter.
My days of dinner
arriving by burly butler
have come to a Level One end.
My (non) performance at group
today has netted me a trip
to the communal dining
room. Mmmmm. Can't wait
to share meat loaf or fish sticks
with a table of friendly, smiling faces.
Like Dahlia's and Lori's.
I wonder how you make friends
with people who think
everyone is out to get them.

What is friendship, anyway?
I have no clue, never
lingered long enough
in one place before,

not with Dad in the military.
We only settled down
in Reno when Mama got so bad
she couldn't find enough white space
to grocery shop or get us to school,
let alone make sure we
bathed and brushed.

Grandma, the fool, stepped up
to the plate, volunteered to look
out for Bryan and me.
Poor woman had no idea what
she was getting herself into—
that Daddy had not only
married a gear shifter
but fathered one too.

I Didn't Realize It Myself

Until a couple of years ago.
Interesting, considering
I'd watched Mom
straddling that seesaw
for as long as I could
remember. Except her highs
and lows lasted for days.
So when I started shifting
gears three or four times
in a twenty-four-hour period,
at first I blamed hormones.

Didn't PMS make
you irritable? Didn't boy
trouble drop you to your knees
(in more ways than one)?
Normal adolescent
feelings, right?
Well, no, see . . . not
when your mother's
a stark raving psycho.
For years she went
undiagnosed.

"Bipolar" had no
meaning when I was
a little girl, and "schizo"
wasn't short for
schizophrenic, not
in the clinical sense.
It only meant that some
days Mama was fine—
eyes not muddied, hair
combed into submission,
speech precise.
Those days, her hugs
and kisses were warm
as summer rain,
washing away the hurt.
The hurt that was sure
to fall again.
We just couldn't guess
exactly when.

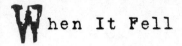hen It Fell

It was a rock slide,
crushing, smothering,
bruising, bone twisting.
By the time I was ten,
I knew to hide when Mama
started talking to the air.

> *Don't worry, Nessa,*
> *He's an angel. Can't you see*
> *him, standing just there?*

I figured if someone was
there, invisible and all,
he must be more demon
than angel, especially
when Mama started yelling.

> *Go away, you bastard. I'm tired*
> *of listening to you.*
> *You make my head hurt.*

That was the thing
about her manic phases.

They didn't always make
her feel what you might
call good. Sometimes
they made her head hurt.

*He's pounding nails
into my brain. Stop!
Make him stop!*

Angel. Demon. Whoever
he was, inside her head,
his pounding made
her rage. Rant. Weep.
Sometimes, to make herself
feel better, she took
to hitting things with her fists.
Walls. Doors. Herself.

Me.

Conner
Ten Days Now

All by myself in this
peppermint green room,
nothing to do but read,
eat, collect lint, reflect

on afternoons lazily
spent, in the arms of my
Emily. Yeah, yeah, I'm
focused. Bent. Obsessed.

I have to see her again,
which means I've got to lie
my way out of here, make
the perfect self-sales pitch.

Dr. Starr will never buy
into "Conner the saint,"
but Dr. Boston might
award me that honor.

I've almost got her right
where I want her—on her
knees, my hands caught in
her silky blond hair as she

whispers, *I want you, Conner.*
Let me chase away thoughts
of your Emily. Come to me
when you get out of this place.

I'll show you how a real
woman makes love to men
such as you, and I don't give
a damn how high the stakes are.

Think it's all smoke and
mirrors? Perhaps. But at
our last session, I noticed
a small lapse of judgment.

It Was Our Second Session

The first session, I'd pouted,
told her nothing except that life
was tough at home, and I
was sick of being controlled.

She didn't give much ground.
Rules are a part of our lives,
Conner. Only children and
fools believe they're immune.

I also noticed her slate
gray eyes and how they kept
assessing me, in an intensely
provocative way.

I mulled that over for two
days, decided it must have
been sexual attraction,
plotted the coming chase.

I arrived at our second
session prepared to win
her sympathy. I opened
my head, bared my brain—

or what was left of it after
a major dose of Prozac.
"When Emily refused to see
me anymore, it almost

broke me in two. I loved
her like Romeo loved his
Juliet, and I know that
lightning won't strike again."

> Her eyes held sympathy.
> *Feeling loss is normal,*
> *Conner. Attempting suicide*
> *isn't dealing with it so well.*

She Wanted to Know

All about Emily, exactly
what made her so outstanding,
so necessary, that I'd rather die
than unknot myself from her.

"She made me feel like the world
turned in my hands, like I could
walk on clouds." Talking about
her, my body churned desire.

Dr. Boston took notice,
on one level or another.
Her own hands trembled,
and she spun her chair toward

the bookcase. When she turned
back around, the top button
on her Jaclyn Smith blouse
had found a way to open.

A hint of cleavage drew
my stare. Why disguise my
obvious interest? I
swear she did it on purpose.

> *Lots of guys lose girlfriends,*
> *Conner. Most just go out and*
> *find someone new. Please try*
> *to trust me enough to explain.*

I closed my eyes, ignoring
both request and décolletage.
"I can't think about her
anymore." Distressed, I stood.

> Dr. Boston rose, neck-
> line dipping. *It's hard to share*
> *secrets. Trade, next time? One*
> *of yours for one of mine.*

Right.

Tony
Today, They Tell Me

My dad is coming to visit.
        Wanting an accounting of
what his money's buying, is
        my best guess. No doubt
he'll be disappointed.
        I'm still just crazy Tony.

I remember the last time
        I saw him. I was nine,
and peeing my pants,
        waiting for the judge
to tell me what a bad
        boy I'd been. Oh yes.

I'd been very bad, and
        Dad stood at the back
of the courtroom, hat
        in hand, a tear in his
eye. 'Course, if he'd
        really cared, I wouldn't

have been there to start
            with. He never once
came to visit after he
            heard my sentence:
Nine years (the max) *in*
            a juvenile detention facility.

They let me out early due to
            good behavior and funding
cutbacks. Seemed the voters
            didn't give two cents about
feeding and schooling hard-
            core kids. Rather than build

bigger facilities, so they could
            lock up more kids longer, as
space was needed, they cut
            delinquents loose early.
Lucky me, they didn't care
            who the kids happened to be.

I Learned a Lot

In juvie, before they sprung
         me. Learned when to shut
my mouth, when to scream;
         how to glom on to the guys
with power, tap into it and
         suck real hard, suck them

inside out. Learned to play—
         sports, people, the system;
learned that there was no
         such thing as love, only
lust. I knew about lust
         already. I'd grown up

immersed in it, and it was
         at the core of my young
incarceration. Ma never
         admitted her part in that,
never even acknowledged
         that the whole thing happened.

Larry is a decent man,
            she said, when I told her
about it the first time.
          A bit rough around the edges,
yes, but he'd never ever
           do such a thing, little liar.

Like an eight-year-old
          child could make up
something so evil and
          perverse. She wouldn't
even believe it when
          I pulled down my jeans.

The proof was right there
          on my underwear, streaked
pink with blood.
             You sat on something,
         that's all. Or maybe you
           did it to yourself. Pig!

Enough Fond Memories

The clock hiccups "two
        forty-five," almost
time for the meet 'n'
        greet with Tony Sr.
Fuck me, what will
        I say? "Hey, Pa, thanks

for making time in your
        busy schedule to drop by once
in the last eight years."
        Part of me wants to turn my
back and walk away, like
        he did, so many years ago.

And what do I remember
        of that day, a major turning
point in my minor life?
        Shouts. Accusations. Denials.
Nothing new, except
        that day, he walked out the door

and never came home,
        except to pack his things,
escorted by a policeman
        to keep him safe from Ma.
He called a few times,
        asked about school, friends.

He sent a birthday present
        once—a baseball glove
and a hardball or two.
        Like I ever had anyone
to play catch with.
        Like I'd ever make a team.

But once Dad decided enough
        was enough, *I* wasn't enough
to make him face the ugly
        truth of Ma. And Tony Jr.
would always remind
        him of her. Severed ties.

Severed me.

Vanessa

Saturday, Visiting Day

Grandma's here, somewhere,
and I'm on my way
to see her. Half of me
feels like I'm walking
a high wire. The other
half feels like I'm fighting
my way through quicksand.

I've missed her so much,
but I don't want to disappoint
her. I mean, I'm not exactly
sane and sober. Definitely
not ready to go back home,
back to school, back to me.
Right now my brain
feels like a soggy sponge.

At the end of the hall,
Dr. Starr shadows
a doorway. *In here,
Vanessa. Your grandmother's
waiting to see you.*

Without meaning to,
I slow my pace,
try to picture Grandma's
face. Will it look exactly
the way it used to—smooth
and pink, despite all
the care it's wrapped around?

Or will she wear
a brand-new set of worry
lines and creases,
and will she look even
older than she is,
because of me?

She's Waiting Just Inside

The door. Definitely a new
wrinkle or two, but she's
beautiful anyway.

> She hugs me into her.
> *How have you been? We've*
> *missed you. Bryan, especially.*

I gulp down guilt.
"I've missed you, too.
And Bryan. How is he?
What's he been up to?"

> She shrugs. *School. A science*
> *fair project. Mostly, he's got*
> *his nose in his books.*

> Dr. Starr allows
> several minutes of small
> talk, finally reels us in, asks us
> to sit opposite each other
> across a narrow table.

*Vanessa has done very
well, at least on the surface.
But sooner or later we'll have
to scratch that surface, crack her
shell, and look inside.*

Grandma's smile falls
away. *Will you want
me here for that?*

Dr. Starr nods. *Eventually.
For some of it, anyway.*

Anxiety deepens Grandma's
creases. Somehow,
she feels responsible.

"Don't worry, Grandma.
You're not to blame.
'Crazy' runs on the other
side of the family."

Grandma's Face Drains

You're not crazy,
Vanessa. You've had
some rough years,
is all. We'll get you
through this and
everything will be just fine.

I want to ask her
if bleach got the
tub white, if Bryan
still has nightmares,
bubbling red with blood.
I want to ask if she
has visited Mama,
where no one wants
to go. Instead I say,
"You're right, Grandma.
We'll come through
fine." Then I ask,
"Have you heard
from Daddy?"

Just got a letter
from Afghanistan.
He couldn't tell me
much, of course.
Rangers keep tight
lips. He's safe but
won't be home any
time soon. He sends
you and Bryan his love.

He always loved
us better from a distance,
especially Mama,
something she found
hard to swallow. So
she found something
easier to swallow.
Which reminds me.
"Does Daddy know

about Mama?"

Trading Secrets

Sounds intriguing, and I
see Dr. Boston again today.
Saturday—no rest for the
wicked, which must include me.

I've been thinking about
her deal. Can the good doctor
have a secret worth knowing—
a true glimpse of the real Dr. B?

I do want to gain her trust.
But first I have to think
about my own secrets,
pretty damn bad to worst.

There is the major one,
really major, in fact, about
Emily, and exactly what kind
of person she happens to be.

There are a couple about
Cara, my evil twin, things
I have done to keep her
out from under my skin.

There is the awful one,
the surrogate mother of all
secrets, you might say. No, I'll
tell *any* other secret but that.

It's psychological
tug-of-war. Finally I
decide the best way out
is to tell her more about

my mad adoration for
a woman twice my age.
I can only hope the
price tag isn't too steep.

My Escort Arrives

Someone short and sour
smelling, someone new—
the weekend shift, no doubt.
No telling who'll open my

       door without knocking next.
       Ready? Dr. Boston is
       waiting. She doesn't offer
       a name, just a steady stare.

I haven't a clue what's
behind that ice-cube gaze.
"Hi, I'm Conner. Would you
mind telling me your name?"

       Can't you read? It's right
       here on my name badge:
       Kate! She's practically
       yelling. Anger? Fear? Of me?

Whatever. I've got my own
fear to deal with. The hallway
buzzes today—kids, adults.
As I veer toward Dr. B's

office, I hear shards of
conversation inside a
conference room. The door
is open, an invitation

> to listen. *Does Daddy know*
> *about Mama?* Such sorrow
> in the voice, I hesitate,
> wanting to find out the answer.

Kate shoves me past before
the reply. Seconds later
a girl sweeps into the hall.
Behind me, I hear her cry

and I turn, wanting to see
her face. It's a gift, despite
the sadness etched there.
What brought her to this place?

No Time to Figure Her Out Now

Dr. B is waiting for me,
a knockout in knockoff
designer suede. The cut
of the suit leaves little doubt

about her luscious figure.
I've got to stop thinking
that way, or I won't have
a shot at controlling

this situation. Maybe I
won't anyway. Hell's bells,
maybe despite my plans
I don't really want control.

> A light must have gone on
> in my eyes, because Dr. B
> suddenly gives me a
> wry smile. *What is it, Conner?*

I shake my head. "Nothing.
Just thinking about control
and how my need for
it seems to be shrinking."

Her smile grows wider.
Oh, I doubt that, Conner.
Now, what did you decide
about confiding secrets?

My eyes lower to the
V of her blouse. "You have
to go first, but I guess I'm
ready to play your game."

> *Okay. When I was younger*
> *than you, but old enough*
> *to know right from wrong,*
> *I had sex with a teacher too.*

She knew?

Tony
Hands Sweating

I walk, heel-touch-toe,
        toward Room C-6
where I'm told I'll find
        Tony Sr. I stroll slowly,
making him wait, like he
        made me wait all this time.

As I round the corner
        Vanessa comes hustling
along the sticky floor,
        eyes glistening. I wonder
what stroke of luck has
        put us both in this space.

"Hey, Vanessa, you
        okay?" She doesn't
look okay, but we won't
        have much time for small
talk before someone
        notices we're here. Alone.

Vanessa sniffles, *Not really,*
but thanks for asking.
Why do they make you
see your family when
all you want to do is
curl up in a little ball?

"They call it therapy,
sweetie. Don't you
feel cured?" I laugh and
she tries too. "I'm
off to see my own warped
next of kin. Feel better."

I start to skip and, a half
smile in her voice, Vanessa
calls, *I already do. And*
Tony? I'll keep my fingers
crossed that things go better
for you than they did for me.

Crossed Fingers

Are not enough. Dread
        sledgehammers my gut
as I approach the door.
        Inside, I hear voices:
Dr. Bellows's grunt and
        a stranger's whine.

The coward in me wants
        to turn around, but screw
him. The kid inside
        wants to see his dad
again, and the avenger
        wants to grill him alive.

I step through the door,
        and the man who turns
to face me looks nothing
        at all like I remember.
His hair is silver—how
        old is he, anyway?—

and his weepy eyes are
        shrunk back into skin
like alligator hide. Will
        I look like this person
one day? He can't really
        be my father, can he?

                    He stands and holds
                            out a hand to me.
                    Hello, Anthony. Long
                            time no see. You sure
                    have changed! How
                            have you been?

All the stuff I wanted
        to say slips from my
brain like oil-slicked
        turds. I stutter, "H-hello,
Pa. I'm okay, I guess."
        I even shake his hand.

I Draw the Line

At hugging him, though.
      Shit, I haven't hugged
anyone since Phillip.
      The last time was in
the hospital, when I
      hugged him good-bye.

Pa tries, and I duck,
      slumping into a chair.
He does likewise, eyes
      never leaving my face.
Then we sit, silent as
      death, until Dr. Bellows says,

> *I gather it's been quite*
>   *a while since the two*
> *of you have seen each*
>   *other. How do you feel*
> *about that, Tony?* He
>   squirms in his own chair.

The question stings
        like alcohol. "You're the
psychologist. How do you
        think it makes me feel?
Deserted. Unworthy.
        Fuck it. I'm pissed."

                Finally, Pa looks away.
                        I'm sorry, Anthony. I
                know I should have been
                        there for you. It was
                a difficult situation,
                        all the way around.

Difficult? For him? My
        hands shake and my
face erupts fire. I struggle
        to find words worthy
of the emotions churning
        inside, in desperate need

of release.

Vanessa

Seeing Grandma

Made me want to go home,
made me want to stay here,
made me miss her and Bryan
and Daddy. Made me scared
to think about Mama again,
and how I left her that day.
Blue. I should be tumbling
low and blue, but instead
I'm swinging the other way.

I'd rather be going blue,
where no eyes can find me.
I think about the eyes I saw today—
Grandma's, hopeful, then nothing
but sad and confused.
Dr. Starr's, ringed
by sleeplessness.
Tony's, a strange jumble
of anticipation and fear.
That other boy's, curious
and intent on me.

Who is he, anyway?
I haven't seen him in group,
not in the cafeteria, not
in the classroom.
He must be new,
new and gorgeous,
the kind of guy every girl
dreams will want her,
but it never quite works
out that way.
So why did he look
like he might
want to get to know me?

There is another pair
of eyes too, eyes
that never saw the light.
Little eyes, that haunt
me deep in the night.

Mania Blossoming

My brain won't quit churning.
I keep seeing pictures, like movies.
Faces. Eyes. Hands. Bodies.
My body, next to Trevor's.
That's what I'm seeing.
He wasn't my first,
wasn't my only, but he
made me feel how
none of the rest could.
How I wish he was here
now, to put out this fire,
this low bank of coals,
smoldering between
my legs. But Trevor
isn't next to me,
never will be again.

I can't deal with your
freaky mood swings,
Vanessa. One minute
you're solid, the next
you're like water.
Boiling water. I love
you. But not enough
to stay with you.

His words were fists,
pounding my belly,
snatching the air from
my lungs. I couldn't talk,
couldn't breathe, so how
could I answer?
He turned his back,
walked away, and I wanted
to die right there.
Instead I went home,
where my hungry
new razor blade
lay in wait.

I Hurried Home That Day

Salivating for steel,
the cold caress of metal, skin
at the mercy of my own hands.
I could still taste Trevor.
He kissed me before he dumped
me, and my mouth held ghosts
of tobacco and Budweiser.
I expected the house to be empty—
Grandma at work and Bryan just
about ready to climb onto
the school bus for an hour ride home.
But when I opened the door,

I heard voices in the kitchen—
one voice, actually. Mama's.

> *You can't hurt me*
> *now, not anymore.*
> *Why couldn't you*
> *just leave me alone?*
> *It's cold here,*
> *very cold. Will it*
> *be like this forever?*

I didn't want her to know
I was there, not while she
was talking to air, but it
was eighty degrees in Grandma's
house. And why was she there,
anyway? I tiptoed toward
the kitchen, peeked around
the doorjamb. Saw her lying
on the floor, an empty pill
bottle near her quiet form.
I walked over, looked down
into her unfocused eyes, saw
something resembling peace.
I should have called 911.
Instead, I backed slowly
away, exited
out the front

door.

Conner

Dr. B Is Psychic?

Or have I given more
away than I can recall?
I lose my smile. "How did
you know? What did I say?"

> *You didn't say a thing.*
> *But Emily Sanders did.*
> *You tried to kill yourself.*
> *What did you think she'd do?*

I never thought that she'd
confess, open herself
to the authorities,
the school board, the press.

> *I'm not surprised you didn't*
> *know. We keep things rather*
> *insular here. But I just*
> *couldn't see us making*
>
> *progress unless you found*
> *out. Since it's all in the*
> *open out there, I hope*
> *you'll talk about it in here.*

I shrug. "Do you want
details? The way she cries
when I kiss her, or how she
never fails to orgasm?

Or maybe you'd like to hear
how sunlight dances, bronze
upon her hair, how she begs me
to pull her hair, to excite her."

> Details, yes. But not like
> those. I want to know how
> you felt after, and why you
> chose a woman twice your age.

She Set Herself Up

"You mean someone like you,
with experience, someone
beautiful and willing? Do
you think it's a myth that guys

my age want to learn how
to please a woman? Sex
with a high school girl is like
screwing a deep freeze."

> *I'm not sure you could*
> *label me "willing," Conner.*
> *But I can't say that I'm*
> *unable to understand*
>
> *an attraction to someone*
> *older. It's true that I*
> *had a relationship with*
> *a teacher, first as a shoulder*
>
> *to cry on when my life*
> *went totally crazy. Caring*
> *turned to passion, but we*
> *never meant for that to happen.*

"It was the exact opposite
for me. At first all I
wanted was sex with her,
but soon I wanted more.

More sex, yes, in unusual
places, and all different kinds.
But that wasn't all. I wanted
her to fill the empty spaces

left by a father who never
once praised me, 'friends' who
used me, an ice princess mom
who raised me with glass kisses."

I Can't Believe

She got me to say all that,
pried open my lips for such
truth to spill out. Dr. Boston
has managed a total eclipse

of Conner the Silent.
Flushed, I chance a glimpse
of her eyes, find sympathy
in their gray, fluid trance.

> *Define 'glass kisses,' Conner.*
> *I want . . . um . . . I don't understand*
> *what you mean.* Nervous hands
> defy her nonchalant tone.

Conner the Silent shrugs, gives
way to Conner the Eclipsed.
"Smooth. Cold. Flawless. Tasteless.
Glass. Agate. Sugarless sorbet."

> She mulls that for a second,
> shakes her head, frees blond
> feathers. *Glass and agate are hard.*
> *Not so sorbet. Please explain.*

My turn to think, to try
and unravel my own riddle.
Every inch of me feels weighted,
like I'm treading gravel.

"My mother is the hardest
woman ever—cool, perfect.
She'd be a diamond, except
you'll never melt one of those.

Sometimes, rarely, influenced
by full moon or emptiness,
she'll rain a single kiss,
monsoon on desert, melting

glass."

Tony

I Want to Jump Up

Leap across the room,
        grab my pa by the neck
and choke him until
        he owns up—confesses
why he can't stand
        the thought of me.

Okay, that's not such
        a great idea, so I shove
it back into my dream
        cabinet, the one I dare
open only when I sleep.
        Lots of bad ideas in there.

Tony? reminds Dr. Bellows.
        Don't you have anything
else to say? Your father
        has come all this way
to try and make some sort
        of amends. Can you do that?

The guy is pissing me
            off. Both of them are,
in fact. I tell myself to stay
            in control, but it won't
be easy. "It's only twenty
            miles from here to Tahoe.

Some people drive
            that far every day. It's
been eight effing years,
            Pa. Don't you own a car?
Or a telephone? What
            the fuck is your problem?

Do you know how
            many nights I lay in bed,
wondering what I'd
            done to deserve your
silence? What had I said?
            What did I ever do, but love you?"

A New Problem Pops Up

One I never expected.
        I can't remember, not
even once in my
        miserable life, crying.
Not when Pa first
        walked out the door.

Not when the judge
        sent me away to live in
a nest of juvenile delinquent
        hornets. Not even the day
I sprinkled Phillip's ashes
        over his secret Truckee

                River fishing hole.
                        So that damn eight-
                pound rainbow who
                        keeps giving me the slip
                will never forget me
                        completely, he requested.

Okay, I almost cried
      that day, tears welling
up black, like thunderheads
      boiling up over the Sierra.
But they never slipped
      down my cheeks, not

like they're doing right
      now. This is totally insane.
All because of this strange
      guy, perched across from me,
this completely strange guy I've
      never really known as my father.

So how can *he* make me
      cry? Why should he even
want to try? "Why now, Pa?
      Why come back into my
life now? Are you hoping
      to become someone's beneficiary?"

Until I Said It

The thought hadn't crossed
        my mind. But now that it has,
I want an answer. "Well?"

                How can you say such a thing,
                      Anthony? No, I don't want one.
                I want to make you mine.

"You think I want your
        money? I've lived just
fine without it up to now."

                Just fine? I know how you
                      live, son. I know where you've
                been, what you've done.

That can't be true, can it?
        Has an invisible eye
been looking my way?

                I can forgive you for all
                      of it, Anthony. The drugs.
                The men. Even the . . . thing.

Now the tears really
        make me mad, chinks
in my invincible armor.

That's a hard thing to
               forgive someone for . . .
to forgive a son for.

Screw it. Tears or no,
          he's got it coming now.
"*You* forgive *me?* I
          didn't turn my back
on you, didn't leave
          you under Ma's thumb.

You knew what she had
          become, what kind of life
that meant for me. Where were
          you, Pa, when I went
hungry? Where were you,
          Pa, when that bastard . . .

never mind."

Vanessa

Prozac Can't Help

Lift me out of the place
I'm in now. Thinking
about my mother always
drops me here, abandons
me clear below mania
into a field of solid blue.
Maybe I should confess
my condition, request a lithium
fix. The Prozac has lately
left me tossing and turning
well into the night.
Then, despite its antidepressant
buzz, I'm tired from staying awake.

Sleepy by day; wound
up at night, brain
fighting my body's need
for REM refreshment.
I suppose I could ask
for sleeping pills, but they'd
drop me way down into the blue,
maybe so deep I could
never crawl back up.
Or I could own up, ask for lith,
but once I start, I can never stop.

And it has side effects, too—
lethargy, weight gain,
massive diarrhea.
(Thirty extra pounds,
despite chronic runs?)

Something else can help,
the thing I crave
more than clarity. Self-
medication—of the most
critical, physical type.
I should wait until after
dinner. Can't go
to the table like Hansel
and Gretel, trailing crumbs
of red. Besides, waiting,
anticipating, can be the best part.

The Dinner Crowd

Seems quite subdued,
the usual chatter strained,
as if no one really wants
to discuss their visit
from home—or lack of one.
Only Stanley seems his usual
obnoxious self—poking
and pushing and asking
the questions no one
wants to answer:

So how did it go?
Any cool news?
Anyone die?
What's your sister look like?

God, he's such a clod.
I go for my plate—fried
chicken, corn, and mashed
potatoes. They definitely
wanted to impress any
parent who might inquire
about tonight's meal, which
is definitely the best I've had
since I've been here—just
enough salt, for once.
As I turn toward the girls'

tables, Tony comes through
the door. I try to catch
his eye, but he keeps both
of them fixed on the floor.

Stanley calls,
Hey, dude. How did it go?
Any cool news?
Hey, man . . .
what's up with your eyes?

Tony glances up, and even
from here I can see
the problem with his eyes—
they're red, swollen,
and that can mean only
one thing, something well
beyond the realm
of Stanley's business.

Tony's Fists Clench

As he turns toward
the offensive lout.
Shut the hell up,
you fat fuck.
I'm sick of you
and your whining shit.

You'd think Stanley
would get the message,
but the idiot dares,
I'm whining? Looks
like you're the one
doing the whining today.

Suddenly the room
moves—guys push
away from their tables,
expecting (hoping for?) a fight.
Girls jump up, move
in for a close-up
view of the action.
Tony is ready to deliver.
I've never seen anyone
so intent on bestowing
a blow or two—or anyone
quite as deserving as

Stanley, who finally
finds some semblance
of brains and says,
Hey man, just kidding.
Besides, if you hit me,
it's back to isolation.

Tony grabs Stanley by
the cheeks, pinches them
pickled beet red.
I don't give two fucks about
isolation, or you. Screw
with me again, you're

dead.

Conner

I Melted Dr. Boston

All those pretty words
worked, just like I wanted
them to. Who knew a poet
lurked inside my brain?

> *I understand better now,*
> said Dr. B. *Thank you,*
> *Conner, for opening up*
> *instead of playing it cool.*

But I did play it cool, and in
the end, she rewarded me
with Level One. I can't
pretend it wasn't my goal.

So I'm on my way to
the dining room, where I'll
sit with hungry lunatics,
all of whom will turn to stare

at the new guy. Paranoid?
No more than I need to be.
Trust is just a five-letter word,
one that comes before "not."

Still, I've got to make Dr. B
believe I trust her completely,
that I, Conner Aaron Sykes,
wear my heart on my sleeve.

> *Don't you feel better with*
> *all of that out in the open?*
> she asked. *Sharing your feelings*
> *is no small accomplishment.*

Despite her corny way
of putting it, I do feel
somehow relieved, like I'm
cutting teeth on psychoanalysis.

I Just Hope

They don't bite one of the hands
that feed them. Speaking of food,
a decent smell drifts toward me,
arousing at least one basic need.

I step through the dining room
door and stumble upon
an interesting scene—a guy
threatening to polish the floor

with a dude three times his
size. Everyone's watching
them, but, as I predicted,
all eyes now rotate toward me.

Catcalls quiet, as if everyone
mistakes me for a member of
the goon squad—where are they,
with the stakes anted this high?

> The smaller guy pushes off
> the fat dude's face. *Don't forget
> what I said, Stanley, and that
> includes messing with my friends.*

He and I need to become
friends. I trail him toward
the serving line as an eerie
silence descends on the room.

A pretty girl—familiar—
with Hershey bar eyes and auburn
hair inserts herself between us.
She and tough guy trade hellos.

> *He had it coming, Tony.*
> *Are you okay? Shall I*
> *assume the outcome of your*
> *visiting day was like mine?*

That Explains a Lot

A visit from home could push
me straight over the edge too—
Tony mumbles something
about his father, fills his plate.

The girl reaches out, covertly
caresses his shoulder, gentle
and warm as September wind.
Tony presses into her touch.

Inexplicably, jealousy
pierces my chest. To be touched
in such a way! I could
easily become obsessed

with this girl. She returns
to her seat, but not before
gifting me with her smile.
Gift? I remember her now—

she's the one I saw earlier,
in the hall. *Hi. I'm Vanessa,*
she says, and I think I could
drown in her husky drawl.

"I—I'm Conner," I sputter,
but she's already gone,
something altogether new
to me—a girl, walking away.

I stare at my fried chicken,
corn, mashed potatoes, not
enough salt, wondering why
Vanessa and Tony mourn

for families, happily
living without them.
Mourning them means
forgiving them, something I'll

never do.

Tony

Cardboard Chicken

Lumpy potatoes, way
        too much salt. It all
tastes like crap, and
        this most definitely
is better than most
        meals in this freak parlor.

Guess I bit the bullet.
        I pretty much expected
a mad rush of orderlies,
        hell-bent on a takedown.
Maybe they were busy
        giving each other head

or maybe they just
        looked the other way.
I bet more than one
        of them would like
to stick a fist in fat
        boy's megamouth.

The mouth in question
        has wisely disappeared
from the room. Everyone
        else has decided to steer
wide of me—everyone,
        that is, except for Vanessa.

She is an angel, and
        she's looking at me
now. Studying me, no
        doubt trying to figure
out what makes the gay
        guy tick. I wish I knew

the answer myself. But
        even if I did know, I
wouldn't tell her. For
        some left-field reason,
I like the idea of her
        trying to figure me out.

The New Dude

Keeps checking me
        out too. Maybe he's
into guys after all, or
        maybe he's trying to
decide whether or not I am.
        All he's gotta do is ask.

        He's sitting with Todd,
                who keeps probing him
        with stupid questions.
                        Hey, man, what's up?
                Ya got a name or what?
                        What are ya in for?

        The name is Conner,
                he says. *Why do you*
        think I'm here?
                        I dunno. Maybe you're
                schizo? You don't
                        look like you use.

Not meth, that's for
        sure. He's way too
buff to be huffing
        that shit, and way
too clear to be cleaning
        himself off downers.

                Conner grins. *I might
                        very well be schizo, but
                    that's not why I'm here.*

                                *Then you musta tried to
                                off yourself. That's
                                        all I can think of.*

            *A very good guess,
                    but it's not something
            I'm ready to talk about.*

        Looks like the new guy
    and I have something
            in common, after all.

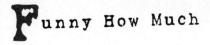unny How Much

You can learn about
        someone, by opening
your ears while they
        talk about themselves.
What did I learn about
        Conner just now?

That the guy is smart,
        maybe almost as smart
as me. That he's strong,
        in control, definitely
more in control than
        I could ever be.

Take, for example,
        my idiotic performance
in front of my father
        today. I should have
stayed cool. Instead
        I crumbled like a cracker.

But that crap about
     forgiveness really blew
me away. I've done
     no more or less than I
needed to, to get by.
     Forgiveness? For what?

And now suddenly
     he appears, like a ghost
materializing from
     out of my forgettable
past—a place I'd rather
     just leave behind.

A place where faces
     wear death masks,
where cold, white
     bodies walk the walk
of zombies, where
     memories jump out,

scream "Boo!"

Vanessa

It's Good to Feel Bad

For someone else, instead
of myself for a change.
Poor Tony looks like he's seen
a ghost. I guess that's how
his dad looked to him.
Funny, Daddy would look
the same way to me.
He has only come home
four times in the last six
years, only stayed a week
or two when he visited.
Each time he's older,
grayer, with meaner eyes,
from seeing all he's seen.

> *Yes, your father knows
> about your mother,*
> Grandma said. *How
> could I keep such
> a thing from him?*

But he doesn't know
about the role I played.
Of course, Grandma
doesn't know either.

She probably wouldn't
believe it if someone
told on me—not that anyone
else has a clue. Only me.
Just another dirty little
secret, a nasty,
filthy secret that won't
quit nibbling at me.
Mama's better off
where she is now,
so why can't I leave
myself alone?

Enough Introspection

I'll focus on something
interesting—like Conner.
In five minutes flat, he put
Todd in his place,
without even being mean.
All he did was straighten
real tall, look Todd
in the eye, and basically
tell him to mind his own business.
You have to admire
his tableside manner.
Not to mention the vivid
aquamarine of his eyes, the wave
of his well-styled hair,
the width of his shoulders.
He catches me staring, smiles,
and I feel like ice cream
on an August sidewalk.

Lori and Dahlia sit nearby,
and they're analyzing him too.

> *He's so cute!* says Lori.
> *How would you like to rub
> up against that?*

Just like a kitty cat,
agrees Dahlia. In fact,
my kitty's purring. Meow!

They are so incredibly gross,
always talking about sex,
as if it's a commodity,
something to be bartered.
I know some people believe
that, and I guess, thinking back
to Trevor and me, I traded
sex for a chance at love.

Breakthrough Moment

That's what Dr. Starr would call
that sudden bit of insight.
Sex, for me, was only
about feeling good
when vines of mania
snared me, pulled me into
this space where my brain
felt so great, my body
didn't want to get left behind.
I can't really blame Trevor
for taking advantage
of that, only for telling
me he loved me. Liar.

> Conner gets up, goes over
> to Tony, extends a hand.
> *I'm Conner. How long*
> *before we have to go*
> *back to our rooms?*

> Tony looks into Conner's
> eyes, as if trying to find
> some ulterior motive.
> He shrugs. *You've got*
> *ten minutes to finish your pie.*

I watch them interact,
and this odd shot
of envy hits. The two
of them are allowed to talk.
But I, being a girl,
am supposed to stay on
"our" side of the room,
when what I'd really like
to do is plant myself between
them. Soak up the warmth of them.
Fall asleep listening to their voices,
snowing down all around me.
To sleep at all tonight,
I'll have to self-medicate.
With a whole different kind

of drug.

Conner

Ten Minutes to Finish

I sit across from Tony,
who's picking at his meringue.
Wonder why I feel like
kicking it with him anyway.

I mean, he's really not
the kind of guy I'd hook up
with at school—not a jock, not
refined, surely not moneyed.

There's just something about
him, something attractive,
but not in a physical way.
On a whim, I tell him,

"They just let me out of my
room today, and I've only
had shrinks to talk to. I feel
like I've escaped from a tomb."

He gives me this strange look,
like he needs to climb inside
my head, walk around in there,
see where that path leads.

Finally he says, *You know
I'm gay*, in a tone that
adds, This is a test. You can
leave if you want. It's okay.

Part of me gets a failing
grade. If I stay, will the
other guys think I want
to get laid—by a dude?

Most of me couldn't care
less about what a bunch
of freaking losers think. Why
try to impress the brain-dead?

Still Another Part of Me

Stresses over a simple fact,
in a major way. I thought
he was attractive. Can
that possibly make *me* gay?

I really don't think so. I mean,
from the time I was twelve
I had an insatiable urge
to climb into the sack

with any girl who would
let me. Then it was older
girls, coeds, who would
seduce a kid simply to get

even with a boyfriend.
Or to play teacher. Cool game.
Finally, it came down
to women, the perfect score.

But men? No, the thought
has never crossed my mind,
except in a voyeuristic way.
Like, does a gay guy *ever*

want to be with a woman?
Which I guess could translate
the other way, which will
continue to stress me a bit.

The weird thing is, Tony
says he's gay and I'm guessing
he really believes it, but he
doesn't seem that way to me.

Anyway, gay or no, something
about Tony has piqued
my interest. So I'll step
out of my homophobic shoes.

Homophobia Stashed

I'll probably have to lie
to pass Tony's litmus test.
"No problem," I tell him. "Some
of my best friends are gay."

> Tony arches an eyebrow.
> *Really? And here I had you*
> *pegged for a total jock.*
> But he smiles freely, and I

realize he's mostly kidding.
I'm up for some fun. "You saying
gay guys can't be jocks? Ever
heard of Dennis Rodman?"

> His laugh breaks whatever
> ice was left between us.
> *Good point. But let me*
> *give you some advice—*

> *never wear a dress to group.*
> *The girls don't even wear*
> *them. Stockings, heels, and*
> *pearls are also on the "don't" list.*

Okay, I like him, can
trust my instincts again.
I notice Vanessa, taking
mental notes, know I must

cozy on up to her, too.
Part of it is my old self,
wanting nectar from a new
flower, the beat of a new heart.

Part of it is a simple need
to connect with someone who
might understand me,
might reach out to imperfect

Conner.

Tony

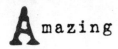
mazing

To find Conner the stud,
        sitting across from me,
trading gay jokes.
        I don't get a gay vibe
from him at all. In fact,
        I notice a probable interest

in Vanessa. Like she's
        'even close to his type!
No, he looks more like
        the sorority/socialite
type. Anyway, I'm
        most likely not his type.

Not that I mind having
        him at my table, literally
or tongue-in-cheek.
        (Where else does Conner
put his tongue? I wonder.)
        Quit! Just go with his flow.

"Did they let you out
        of isolation already?
That was pretty quick."

Was it? Well, it seemed
like a long damn time
to me—eight days.

"That's not so bad.
          They kept me locked
up for two weeks."

Two frigging weeks,
pacing that room, I'd
be a basket case by now.

"You must have worked
          some kind of magic.
Eight days is cake."

Conner grins. Magic,
yeah, that's it. I put Dr.
Boston under my spell.

I Don't Doubt That at All

The Black Widow
        believes she's a player.
But players are easily
        played by better players,
someone, for instance,
        of Conner's caliber.

"Yeah, well, what about
        Dr. Starr? You'll have to
work voodoo on her."

                        She's a special case, okay.
                        Voodoo, huh? Have a
                        couple strands of her hair?

"Shee-it! I wouldn't
        touch that greasy gray hair
with Stanley's fingers."

                        Good point. And speaking
                        of Stanley, what's his story?
                        Can't be meth, that's for sure.

"Definitely not crystal.
        Rumor has it he tried
to kill his little brother."

Conner's smile vanishes.
No shit? They let total
nutcases in here, huh?

"Enough money can buy
     a total free ride. His parents
were just a little short."

                    More likely they wanted
                 him locked up somewhere.
                      Just not behind real bars.

An Excellent Observation

One I consider as I give
        my plate to the girls working
kitchen duty. No, there aren't
        always girls in there—this
just happens to be their
        week to play Martha Stewart.

One thing I'll say,
        chauvinistic or not,
the girls are much better
        cooks. As far as dish
washing, I can't see that
        gender makes a difference.

The dining room buzzes
        with after-dinner activity.
The goon squad stands
        by, making sure everyone
heads in the right direction—
        rec room or bedroom,

depending on what level
        they've achieved. Dr.
Starr awarded me Level
        Two, so I get my choice.
This is a favorite time
        for a little male-female

interaction, and Conner
        takes total advantage,
moving in on Vanessa
        before Kate or Paul
can get the chance
        to move in on him.

As they wander toward
        the door, he whispers
something in her ear.
        I'm not close enough
to hear, but I'm close
        enough to notice her

blush.

Vanessa

Credit Where It's Due

I've got to hand it to Conner.
He walked into a room
that hovered on the brink
of chaos, and the simple
weight of his entrance
seemed to put everything right.

Tony didn't hit Stanley,
didn't wind up in isolation.
Stanley left the room
in what would have been
a state of shame for anyone
who could feel ashamed.
I think he mostly felt lucky
to have survived the incident
with only the slightest hint
of a bruise on either cheek.

Then Conner had the nerve
to go sit with Tony,
who was stewing alone
at the back of the room.

He even joked him into smiling,
something I couldn't do.
Now, as we get ready
to go back to our rooms,
close ourselves in, fall
into our lonely vigils,
he comes to me, touches
the small of my back.

Then he whispers, *I just
want you to know you light
up this dingy room.*

Yeah, I know it's a line.
But it makes my face heat
up—and something else, too—
in a very good way.

I Play It Cool

As if boys say stuff like that to me
all the time—no big deal, right?
I whisper back a plain-
Jane, "Thank you"
but don't dare turn around,
show him how red
my face has grown, a clear
indication that I am not used
to such compliments.

> I think the best thing Trevor
> ever said to me was,
> *You're pretty cute,*
> *with your clothes off.*

Clothes off is actually
the worst view of me,
a few too many pounds
of flab, in all the wrong
places (i.e., my thighs,
but not my breasts).
Of course, Grandma says
I'm just right, a perfect
size seven. Size three
would be preferable.

Still, I feel almost desirable,
with Conner's breath
against my neck, his voice
like a warm wind in my ear.
At the very least, he's pulled
me way up out of the blue,
into a new bloom of white.
Two swings in one day.
Something is majorly
going on.

In the Refuge of My Room

I almost decide sleeplessness
is better than the monster,
come knocking at the little
door smack in the middle
of my forehead, begging
for a teaspoon of Prozac.
I know what I have to do
but don't quite know how to do it.
They check my stitches,
make sure they're not infected.
Or messed with.

> *Wouldn't want to come in*
> *and find your hand hanging*
> *by threads again,* the nurse
> told me once.

I don't want that either.
But I do need release.
I've saved my "secret weapon"
for a night like tonight,
when nothing else will suffice.

I borrowed it from Dr. Bellows's
desk one day, when his attention
turned to a ring of his cell phone,
stashed in his briefcase on the floor.
The paper clip sat in plain sight,
almost an invitation.

I retrieve it from my hiding
place, beneath the leg of my bed.
It's cool and comforting in my hand
as I slowly unfold it, test
its semisharp point with one finger.
Careful not to probe
too deeply, draw too much attention,
I insert it just below the skin
of my right wrist, down
into a single blue vein.
Oh God! Not enough!
Easy now, right to left,
vein to vein, connect

the dots.

Life Isn't Fair

My dad has told me that
at least a hundred times.
Life isn't fair, and luck?
That is something you create.

He's spent forty-five years,
creating a monster stash
of luck, working twelve-hour
days, hating every minute

he had to devote to problems
at home. Mom isn't much
better, but at least she can
remain calm when everything

turns ugly—like the day
I spurted blood on her new
Berber carpeting. Amazing,
how she skirted the puddle,

staunched the flow with a towel,
and barely touched me at all—
didn't dare stain the Versace.
Mom rarely touched Cara

or me, though, not even when
we were spotless. Diaper
changing and bubble baths she
left in the hands of our nanny.

Leona pulled "Mommy" duty
until Cara and I turned
fourteen. She was plump, pretty,
and I will always remember

her with a love far beyond
what a child might feel for his
substitute mother. When Leona
smiled, all was right in my world.

The Memory Stirs Sadness

It scatters around me like dust.
My heart beats against
the dent in my chest and I
feel far apart from the things

in my life that brought me
to this place. My evening
meds have yet to kick in.
I get out of the chair, pace.

One, two, three, four, halfway to the piss green wall.
Five, six, seven, eight. Pivot,
hit replay. One, two, three . . .

It occurs to me that just
hours ago, all I wanted
was to get out of here,
to crawl back to Emily.

I planned on trumping her
with the guilt card, showing
her how a .22 bullet had
scarred both body and psyche.

But now I don't think she'll
see me. Won't open the door
or answer the phone, which
leaves only my family

to go home to. I know
I'm not ready for that.
Suddenly I find myself
caught by a wave of nausea.

Was it the chicken? I fall
on the bed, close my eyes,
hope the churning wake
will vacate my head, let me

sleep.

Tony
Sunday Morning

I slide into a clean
        pair of black jeans,
a button-up blue
        work shirt. Comb
my hair, brush my
        teeth, ready for God.

But is He ready
        for me? Funny, but
the person who gave
        me my first real taste
of the Good Lord
        was dear, gay Phillip.

"Do you really believe
        in an all-powerful Creator?"
I asked him, one Sunday
        morning, a year or so
ago. "And in some place
        we go after we die?"

I do, indeed. I can't
             say exactly what
He is, or where
             Heaven might be.
But I believe there's
             a place there for me.

It made no sense at all
             to me, but I followed
Phillip to church that
             morning, and something
(Someone?) there
             spoke to my heart.

You're safe here, it
             (He?) said. No judgments,
no worries, you're
             one of My children,
and a special part
             of the Grand Plan.

Okay, It Sounds

Like some weird
       soap opera. But that's
what I heard, or maybe
       I felt it. I don't know.
Don't care. And hey,
       if I'm wrong, nothing lost.

It does comfort me
       to think there might
be something after
       we close our eyes
for the final time—
       a light to walk toward.

I hope Phillip took
       that walk. According
to the Book, all that's
       required is faith. He
believed, so he should
       be There, waiting for me.

"But what about being
       gay?" I asked Phillip once.
"Some say that dooms you."

> *I think God cares more*
> *about how you treat others*
> *than who you sleep with.*

Which worries me some.
        I did once mistreat
a man about as bad
        as you could do someone.
Though I asked Him
        for forgiveness, maybe

I don't deserve it,
        because I don't feel
even a little bit bad
        about what I did.
I know He knows why.
        I only hope it matters.

I Also Hope

He understands why I
        tried to kill myself
and that He doesn't
        turn His back if I one
day succeed. Surely
        that's better than taking

up room on this dying
        planet, when so little
room is left. The hardest
        part about this religion
thing is that every "believer"
        believes something different.

Anyway, I don't really
        believe like this visiting
chaplain does. He's pure
        hellfire and brimstone—
too Baptist for my taste.
        Oh yeah, I know Baptists,

Catholics, too. I sampled
            both along the way, in
deference to the two
            sides of my family.
Ma wasn't a churchgoer,
            obviously, but her ma

was a Texas Southern
            Baptist who took me to
a revival or two when
            we went to visit once.
Holy rollers! Who could
            qualify for *their* Heaven?

Pa's people were Pope
            lovers, and the Vatican
view of right or wrong
            leaves me reeling too.
I bet Pa's at mass right
            now, spouting Hail Marys

for me.

Vanessa

I'm Told Level One

Means Sunday services,
an hour or more being scared
silly by some volunteer preacher.
They even make the little kids go.
Church didn't used to scare me.
But that was before
Mama introduced
me to her angel. He was so real
to her, I used to wonder
why I couldn't see or hear him,

> when Mama could.
> *Plain as day.*
> *And if you can't hear*
> *him, little girl, it means*
> *you haven't qualified*
> *to enter the pearly gates.*
> *You'd better ask for forgiveness.*

She never said what for,
but she sat me at the table
with a dog-eared King James,
made me read for hours. Out loud.

There's that other thing, too.
Most women in that situation
move on with their lives.
No second thoughts. No guilt.
Most other women aren't me.
I did ask for forgiveness then.
Still don't know His answer.

My bad wrist throbs,
and my good one pulses
pleasant memories of a paper clip.
One more little poke couldn't hurt.
I tiptoe to the door, listen
for movement in the hall.
No footsteps.
Out comes my little friend.
This time I insert it just behind
my knee, where a long skirt
will cover it so no one
but God can see.

A Long Flowing Skirt

And a long-sleeved blouse
disguise all signs of SI—no,
not *Sports Illustrated*.
SI stands for self-injury,
another term I learned
surfing the Web. The best
thing about those boards
and blogs is knowing
I'm not alone.

> *I cut to focus when my*
> *brain is racing.*
> *I cut to make physical*
> *what I feel inside.*
> *I cut to see blood*
> *because I like it.*
> *I don't like to cut,*
> *but I can't give it up.*

I have felt all those things,
cut for all those reasons.
But now I cut for another,
much more substantial reason.

I cut when I think I hear
a baby crying. When I think
I hear Mama calling.
Knowing those things
are impossible but hearing
them just the same.
And that's something
I'll never break down
and admit to anyone
but myself.
Bipolar crazy is one thing.
Schizophrenic is another.
Could I have inherited both?

I Sit at the Back

Of the dining-room-turned-
chapel. It's the only room
big enough to accommodate
all of us. And attendance
is mandatory. Do they really
think they're saving souls?
If so, my suggestion
would be not to bother.
In my admittedly
limited knowledge of religion,
desire to change is a requirement.

Glancing around the room,
I can find only a few
who might qualify.
Justin, of course.
A couple of girls whose
names I don't know,
with beatific grins
lighting their plain faces.
And—this is weird—Tony,
who's sitting two rows up.
It seems to me that "gay"
and "God" make strange
bedfellows, in the most
figurative sense, of course.

But Tony seems caught up
in the drama of the morning—
singing hymns, praying
the Our Father, listening
raptly to the sermon, a ramble
straight out of Revelations.
There's a lot more to Tony
than what's on the surface,
that's for sure.
Wonder how deep I'd
have to dig to find

it all.

Conner
Mandatory Church Services

What other surprises does
Level One have in store?
I don't believe in God,
don't believe in the devil.

Unless you want to count
my mother. She might be
Satan's sister, I suppose.
What other explanation

could there be for someone
sizzling hot on the outside,
yet frozen solid beneath
the skin. Not quite human.

Anyway, I get to wear
my wrinkled Ralph Lauren.
It's worse than I thought,
having stayed crinkled against

the back of the drawer
going on a dozen days now.
At least my Dockers aren't
showing signs of mistreatment.

Whatever. It's good to be
out of sweats, feeling half
human again. I arrive just
as the minister says, *Let's*

> *get started. Turn your eyes*
> *to the Lord, fill your hearts*
> *with gladness, reach out for*
> *your heavenly reward.*

He's a poster board preacher
and I hate him already.
I spy an empty chair in
back, suddenly glad I'm late.

I Sit Beside Vanessa

I can't believe the chump
on my right left a place
next to her for me. I settle
in as the brainwashed recite

> a well-worn prayer, not
> completely foreign to me:
> *Our father, who art in heaven,*
> *hallowed be thy name . . .*

It's not like I've never
been to church before.
My parents make us go
on holidays, fighting sin

twice every year—the day
Mary gave birth, the day
her son died, so the stories
go. All to save me? Right.

> Vanessa leans over,
> sweeping my cheek with
> an auburn wisp. *I'd rather*
> *be sleeping,* she whispers.

She smells of industrial-
strength soap, but so do I.
At least we're clean. I notice
the length of her skirt,

which covers too much, if
you ask me. One slender
arm comes to rest on one
knee, and at the wrist, a few

drops of blood, scarlet
clues to the mystery
that is Vanessa. I lean
back, watch her secret ooze.

After the Last Amen

We're allowed some time
to mingle, guys and girls
together as if, now holy, not
a single indecent thought

could cross our commingled
minds. Vanessa's knee brushes
mine, raising some quite improper
thoughts. A voice reminds

> me we're not exactly alone.
> *Good morning! Hope I'm
> not interrupting.* Tony's eyes
> fall, a warning to Vanessa

to hide her wrist. But she
doesn't, maybe because
she doesn't care, or maybe
she just doesn't see.

> He reaches out, touches
> her arm. *What's this, sweet
> lady?* He disguises concern
> with charm. Unexpected.

Vanessa snatches her arm
away. *Nothing. No worries.*
I poked myself with a fingernail.
Her eyes betray the lie.

Tony and I exchange
a glance, brimming with disbelief.
But we know it's a delicate
dance and keep our mouths

shut.

Tony

Vanessa's Cutting

And the only thing I can
        do is point it out to someone
in charge—betray her
        to the enemy. Not really
an option. I wouldn't
        want her to tell on me.

So I shrug. "Hope it doesn't
        get infected. You should
clip those fingernails!"

                Yes, Mother. I'll put it
                    near the top of my list.
                Right after flossing.

        Conner asks, *Are Sunday*
            services really required?
        What happens if you
            say you won't come?
        Will they lock you up,
            throw away the key?

"They'd drop you back
        down a level," I answer,
as the resident expert.

Back to being a big
           zero, Vanessa says.
Back to isolation.

"Only if you're Level
        One. But hey, lucky
me, I've been promoted
        to Level Two. Just
wait. You get to play
        pool, get to watch TV."

           No kidding? says Conner.
                   And what do you get
           for making Level Three?

Level Three Privileges

"From what I hear,
          you get trips to the mall,
movies, sometimes,
          always well supervised.
You also get to go home
          for weekend visits."

                    Maybe I'll just skip
                              Level Three, Conner
                    comments. *Level Four?*
"That's the wilderness
          camp—Challenge by
Choice, they call it."

                    Vanessa chimes in, *If you*
                              complete the Challenge,
                    you get Level Five.
"And that," I add,
          "is when they let you
out of here for good."

Sounds like it would
        be easier to wait it out
until I turn eighteen,
        Conner observes. *Not*
so long, only six months,
        two weeks, three days.

Speak for yourself, says
        Vanessa. *It's eleven months*
until my birthday. And
        I don't plan to celebrate
that party in here! I'll
        be out long before then.

"They'll probably kick me
        out next week," I say. "I gave
my dad hell yesterday,
        and he's footing the bill.
'Course, I've got his guilt
        train steaming real good."

Time to Vacate

The room, so they can
        turn it back into a place
to eat lunch. I volunteer
        to help. Nothing better
to do than fold down tables,
        set chairs around them.

Conner has apparently
        digested our recent
conversation, because
        he volunteers to help
too. Anything extra you
        do goes in the "plus column."

Vanessa doesn't dare.
        Someone might notice
the seep on her wrist.
        Someone less discreet
than Conner or me.
        We watch her hustle off.

"That girl is something
        special," I say. "Wonder
what her story is."

Other than cutting
herself, you mean?
The why behind the blade?

"Exactly. She seems so
grounded, compared
to other losers in here."

I might say the same about
you. But you tried to off
yourself too. Didn't you?

"Yep. Failed miserably,
too. Some things take
practice. Suicide, for one."

Conner laughs. *You're*
right. And who knew?
Next time I'll be more

careful.

Vanessa

All This Talk

About reaching levels
and getting out of this place
makes me want to put myself
on a fast track to freedom.
I guess that means opening
up in group, succeeding
in school, which I started
again last week, hopeful
I might catch up after missing
so much.

I hadn't even cracked
a book in over a month.
Magazines, yes. Plenty
of those in the hospital,
and I've borrowed a *Cosmo*
or two from my pal Dahlia.
Pretty tame stuff, for her.
Hustler is more her style.

I've seen a couple of those,
thanks to darling Trevor,
who five-finger-discounted
them from the local liquor store.

I can't believe women
would let themselves be photographed
like that! Nothing "artsy"
about fake rape scenes or lying naked
with a dog. It's pure nasty.
And all for money.

I'm not sure what I want
to do for money when
it's up to me to make it.
Not sure what I can do,
bouncing white to blue.
But I don't plan to use my body
to make it. I plan to use
my bipolar brain.

Monday Morning

Up early, shower, breakfast
at seven thirty. Not so different
from living at home, except
none of it is by choice,
everything choreographed,
right down to the soap
we use, the toothpaste
we're allowed, the exact
amount of eggs on our plates.
It's easy, really. Easy
and frustrating.

Classes, remedial for many here,
start at nine. Lucky me.
The month off didn't put me
too far behind, which means
I get to be with the advanced
group, and that includes Tony.
He's book smart. Street smart.
I never knew for sure the two
could go together, but they're
intertwined, inside of him.
The more I get to know him,
the more I like him.
My first gay friend.

I've never really had much
in the way of friends before.
A few little girlfriends,
army brats all, and tough
to keep when you change
bases like clothes.
But I'm pretty much stuck
here for a while. A friend
seems like a good thing
to have, and I think I have two.
Tony. And Conner.
Cute. And devastating.
A daunting duo.

They're Both in Class

Of course Conner would
be in the advanced class.
He's college prep all the way.
Maybe he can tutor me
in the fine art of finesse.
Girls sit on one side
of the classroom,
guys on the other,
in alphabetical order.
Easier to keep track of.
Guess Mr. Hidalgo
isn't as smart as his students.

> *Good morning, all*, he says.
> *Today, we're writing essays.*
> *Topic: The Patriot Act,*
> *right, wrong, or indifferent.*

A half-dozen groans
answer his request, but
I like putting my opinion
on paper for the world to read.
Conner raises his hand.

Excuse me, sir, but can
you tell us, please, how
the Patriot Act affects
the rights of minors?
I mean, we were basically
locked up here without
a hint of "due process."
How is that any different
than treading all over
the due process of
a so-called adult?

Mr. Hidalgo clears his throat,
considers how to answer
a student as impertinent—
yet polite and somehow
correct, in context—as

Conner.

Conner

Okay, I Should Have

Kept my mouth shut, gone
with the flow, especially
the first day in Mr. Hidalgo's
class. But I need to know

what makes every teacher
tick. Some really care about
their students' reasoning
processes. Others just stick

to the three Rs—rote
learning, recitation,
rhetoric. In here, I didn't
expect to find a discerning

teacher. But Mr. Hidalgo
does seem pretty reasonable.
He even allowed me
to expand on the theme

"due process and minors."
Why do I care, anyway?
"Life" has lately not meant
much. I haven't a clue why

"liberty" should concern me.
Like I've ever really been
free? (Or ever could be.)
Whatever. At least I've got

something to do besides
pace my room. I start to
write, in a perfect hand
so I won't have to erase.

One thing I won't stand for
is a sloppy paper, and I
refuse to write a first draft,
then have to copy over.

Duplicating Effort

Is a true waste of time,
one I watch others take
unusual pride in—spilling
mistakes, which must be undone

before turning in their papers.
Why not just do it right
the first time? Working around
the knot in my neck, I write:

Our forefathers envisioned
the Bill of Rights as a safety
net—necessary corrections
of the Constitution's oversights.

But where did they write that one
must be at least eighteen for
those rules to apply? Would they
have found such a provision just,

when many patriots of the day,
who died in the name of freedom,
were themselves only boys?
I've made the same argument

before, in a different
school, with another teacher.
Like her, Mr. Hidalgo
is cool with my opinion.

> *You've made some excellent*
> *observations, and conveyed*
> *your thoughts clearly. I have*
> *high expectations of you.*

High expectations—great,
I burned myself again.
You'd think by now I would
have learned to underachieve.

Especially in Here

Where underachievement
is an art. Not that success
isn't possible for these
people, that they're not smart.

If Justin could just get past
his Jesus fetish, he'd
likely be an algebra
whiz, but such linear

thinking conflicts with his
four-dimensional ideals.
Then there's Nathan, whose
unconventional theories

about extraterrestrial
visitation defy known
laws of science: E.T.,
the brains behind creation.

Tony, at least, is rooted
in reality, tinted as his
view might be, intertwined
with his iffy sexuality.

He puts his words on paper
well; writes with clarity
and passion; is not afraid
to tell us how he feels:

> *Freedom is a double-edged*
> *ideal, because true freedom*
> *comes without the protection*
> *of laws that also enslave us*
>
> *by defining us—female,*
> *male; Christian, Islamic;*
> *good, evil. All at the whim*
> *of a frail minority.*

Right on.

Tony

An Odd Thing Happened

When I started school
        here, at Aspen Springs.
I found out I'm good
        at it. I never was before.
Of course, I never had
        much chance to excel

in the juvenile detention
        center. Anything I learned
was because I wanted to,
        not because someone
expected me to. I'd be
        a total ignoramus

if not for Phillip.
        Now *he* expected
great things from me.
        And being an ex-college
professor, he was just
        the gentleman to teach me.

He taught me the basics—
        algebra, biology, U.S. history.
He taught me the extras—
        trig, chemistry, world affairs.
He taught me the necessities—
        philosophy, religion, psychology.

I could have learned from
        him forever. But we didn't
have forever, only two
        almost-perfect years,
years that might have
        been perfectly perfect

except he got so sick. I'm
        not sure how I've managed
to avoid that whole vicious
        viral thing. Then again,
maybe I haven't. I can
        only wait and see.

Anyway, I Don't Worry

About it, not on a daily
            basis. The weird thing
is, I don't really worry
            about much anymore,
not with Phillip gone.
            That was my biggest worry

for the last couple of years.
            I had no idea what I'd do
when he died. He had put
            me in his will, but his son
contested and won, claiming
            his house and every possession.

Yes, Phillip was married
            once, back when most gay
men remained in the closet,
            at least to family and friends,
taking their need to be with
            other men to the darker parts

of town—bath houses,
          bars, back alleys, and cars.
No wonder AIDS spread
          like it did. Everyone was
afraid to talk about it.
          What if the wife found out?

Phillip was one of the brave
          ones who couldn't stand
sneaking around. So he
          told his wife, who promptly
ran off to tell her priest
          and get a divorce, in that order.

Poor Phillip lost his wife,
          his son, his friends, and his
church, all within a few
          days. Luckily, the university
where he taught was in San
          Francisco. At least he kept his job.

Mr. Hidalgo
Clears His Throat

Brings me back to my
        essay: "The Patriot Act,
Who Cares?" I write:
        I think it's totally messed
up that cops can arrest
        anyone they want, just

because they don't like
        how a person looks. But
what, exactly, is so new
        about that? The only
difference I can see under
        the Patriot Act is the authorities

don't have to tell anyone
        they've busted the guy.
They can keep him for days,
        even weeks, and no one
who cares about him will
        know where he's gone.

They call that patriotism?
        And wiretaps? Or investigating
what a person reads? Who,
        then, gets to decide what
reading materials constitute
        terrorist training guides?

When will America quit
        living in the shadow
of 9/11? When will her
        people decide to stop
living in daily fear?
        When will they think

twice about who they
        should be afraid of—
some would-be terrorist
        a thousand miles away,
or some U.S. politician, hell-
        bent on peeking behind

        closed doors?

Vanessa

Writing Essays

Is usually easy for me.
But I'm having a hard time
with this one, for a couple
of reasons. The first is Daddy,
who's been fighting terrorists
on their own turf ever since
9/11 went down.
Ask him, the Patriot Act
doesn't do nearly enough
to keep America safe.
Ask him, he'd send every
"damn towelhead"
back to where they came from,
with a stop at Guantanamo
for a little debriefing.

The second is Grandma,
who is quite vocal about
patient confidentiality
and the need to keep medical
records inviolable.
I know I wouldn't want
just anybody to be able
to take a look at mine.

Nope, no job for Vanessa.
She's crazy, you know.

I may very well be crazy,
but the manager at McDonald's
doesn't need
that information to decide
if I'm safe to flip burgers.
Not like I'd freak out and off
someone because he complained
the fries were greasy.
At least, I don't think so.

The Third Reason Is Mama

Everything always comes back
to her, doesn't it?
Plenty of times, tripping
around town, no meds to stabilize
her schizophrenic mood shifts,
she looked like a regular
lunatic—the kind that sleeps
in the park, digging through
trash cans for dinner
and talking to pigeons
like they can talk back.
In fact, she did all those things.

Sometimes cops will look
the other way. Other times,
bad day or whatever, they decide
to roust "the wackos,"
rough them up, haul them in,
whatever their mood dictates.
Once in a while, if the wacko
takes offense and puts up
some sort of a defense,
the cop goes overboard.
More than once, Mama
came home with bruises.

But what if one of those
times, she never came
home at all, and no one
knew where she'd been
taken to? She's got red hair,
green eyes, no ties to the Middle
East. But under the Patriot
Act, everyone is fair game.

I have no problem with
increasing security to keep
this country safe.
But how do we decide
who poses a threat?
And—bigger question—
who decides?

Mr. Hidalgo Comes Over

You haven't written anything,
Vanessa. Having a hard time
getting started?

I could tell him everything
I've just been thinking,
but that would take us all
the way to lunch. "Just
organizing my thoughts.
I tend to do most of my
writing inside my head."

He smiles. *Okay. But don't*
let it get lost inside there.
I'd like a first draft today.

I glance around
the classroom. Conner
is already finished.
I can tell by the satisfied
expression on his face.
Tony is scribbling away.
Guess he knows what
he wants to say.

Others are chewing
pencils, staring off
into space. I don't want
to look as scattered
as they do, so I start:

> Once we believed ourselves
> safe from attack, here on our
> home turf, hallowed ground.
> The events that occurred
> on September 11, 2001,
> altered our "pie in the sky"
> view. The sad fact is, no one
> is completely safe. We're all
> going to die someday. What's
> important is how we choose
> to live until the day of our judgment
>
> comes. . . .

Conner

Six Weeks in Aspen Springs

The doctors say I'm making
progress, however they
define that. I'm mostly
over Emily, I guess,

so something inside me
has changed. I no longer
feel mad with desire for her,
deranged by my inability

to see her, talk to her. I
haven't heard what happened
after she broke down, admitted
guilt. Not a single word,

though I've begged Dr. Boston
to ignore the rules, confide
details of Em's self-imposed
destruction. Despite our rapport,

she maintains, *You know I can't
do that, Conner. It could
adversely affect your therapy.
Please don't pursue this further.*

Once I even went so far as
to reach across her desk,
rest my hand lightly on hers,
and say, "Then teach me how

not to care about someone
who was everything to me.
All I want is to know she's
okay. Is that too much to ask?"

She flinched but didn't move
her hand. *No. But it's more
important that we talk
about you. Understand?*

The Only Way

To find my answers, learn
anything more, is to do
what it takes to let Level
Three take me out the front door.

Even supervised outings
should give me the chance
to make a covert phone call.
Until then, I'll play "good."

I've swallowed most of my
pride, dressed down in sweats,
showered naked with creeps,
some of them way too obsessed

with checking out other guys.
It's worse than any football
locker room, because while
jocks can be crude, perverse

even, they all have girlfriends
waiting outside. These losers
have no one but each other,
one reason I haven't tried

to buddy up too close.
Still, I stay cordial. No
need to make enemies.
Besides, halfway going

along with the Aspen Springs
game plan has netted me
Level Two. Unimpressive.
Funny, I never regretted not

learning Ping-Pong until
now. Even Stanley can beat
me, and I haven't a clue
how—he's too fat to move fast,

so it must have more to do
with spin. Whatever. Losing
every game to Stanley
is beginning to wear thin.

So I'm Pushing Hard

To graduate to Level
Three. I've kept my nose
to the grindstone in school,
stroked my way past Dr. B.

Now I've just got to convince
Dr. Starr. The bulldog is
waiting for me right now,
sitting as far back from

the patient's chair as the wall
will allow, as if "suicidal"
were contagious. Working
the bulldog takes more than skill.

It takes subtlety. "Good
afternoon, Dr. Starr. You
look lovely in that shade
of maroon." Okay, not great.

She grimaces. *Let's get down
to business, Mr. Sykes.
When we last left off, we
were discussing your sister.*

I don't want to talk about
Cara, but we're playing
by Dr. Starr's rule book.
I shut my eyes, see my twin's

face, so like my own—soft,
toffee brown hair; startling
hazel eyes; skin the color
of coffee with lots of cream.

"She's really very beautiful.
Takes after our mother,
outside and in. Meaning
she's a bitch." My heart aches,

remembering.

Tony

Commotion in the Hall

Voices. Shouts. Shuffling
        feet and the scratch of claws
against linoleum. Dogs
        can mean only one thing—
a drug search. I stick my
        head out the door, looking

for the source of all this
        excitement. Uniforms,
with real guns attached.
        Two German shepherds,
sniffing along the
        corridor, asking to go

inside rooms which, one
        by one, empty. Guys,
some half-dressed.
        Girls, ditto. Which most
definitely makes an
        impression on the guys.

                Hey, Dahlia, calls dim-
                        wad Stanley. *Nice pair
                of tits you got there.*

Hey, Stanley, she
                    yells back. *Same to you,*
but more of them!

Despite the situation,
            everyone has to laugh.
Everyone, that is, except
            Todd, who has just been
led out of his room,
            face in his metal-cuffed

hands, by a tall deputy
            and a short German
shepherd. I thought
            he seemed buzzed
the last time I saw him,
            but didn't go there at all.

As Todd Is Marched Away

The search continues.
        He may have shared
his contraband, after
        all. Meanwhile, Paul
and Kate appear. Half-
        dressed or fully clothed,

we're herded toward
        the dining room, where
we're instructed to wait
        until the operation is
over. A sting, in Reno's
        premier RTC—residential

treatment center.
        The press will love
this one, not that it's
        so uncommon. I've even
seen drugs delivered
        to inmates at the juvenile

detention center—
        left by a Dumpster
within semi-easy
        reach behind the chain-
link fence surrounding
        the exercise yard.

Paul and Kate pace
        nervous circles around
the loosely grouped
        Aspen Springs flakes.
Out in the hallway,
        I hear the muffled

voices of the younger
        kids—all under twelve—
who live in a different
        wing. Most of them have
suffered abuse: physical,
        sexual, or (please specify) other.

Which Takes Me Back

Home to Ma, a string
        of "uncles" and their
friends. Reno, small
        as it is, is home to a wide
variety of perverts.
        Think how many there

must be on this poor,
        sick planet! The worst
part is, since scientists
        tell us perverts beget
perverts, you almost
        have to feel sorry for them.

Perverts aren't born—
        they're created. I wish
I could give every kid
        the kind of childhood
I didn't have—one filled
        with toys, warmth, love.

Speaking of love,
      here comes Vanessa.
Not only do I love
      her, but, funny as it
sounds, I think I'm
      in love with her. Crazy!

But how else can I
      explain the way I break
out in a sweat when
      she's near, the way
I look for opportunities
      to make that happen?

              Hey, Tony, she almost
                    sighs. *Too bad about*
              Todd, huh? I thought
                    he was over all that.
And as she talks, I
      shiver at a cool hint

of sweat.

Vanessa

I Watch Tony

Listen to the voices
of the little kids, out in the hall.
A strange expression creeps
across his face. I wonder
what he's thinking,
but my intuition whispers
it's one of those things
he'd rather not talk about.
At least not yet.

So I make small talk
about Todd. "It's sad how
people give their lives
to meth. I mean, if you're
going to kill yourself,
there are faster ways
than letting something
chew up your brain
one lobe at a time."

Tony shrugs. *Do enough*
crank, your heart will give
up before your brain does.
Most people don't
do enough to die, though.
They just do enough
to keep getting more
and more stupid.

"Like stupid enough
to smuggle meth into
a place like this?"

Exactly. What was
the guy thinking?
Now he'll do serious
lockup, and that
ain't pretty. Trust me.

The Funny Thing Is

I do trust Tony. But why?
A gay guy, from the wrong
side of town, who I only
met a few weeks ago?
Why do I feel like
I've known him forever?
Were we friends
in another lifetime?
I've read about reincarnation.
(Had to hide the books so
Mama wouldn't find them—
she'd have skinned me alive!)
It doesn't sound so unreasonable.
So I ask, "Do you believe
in reincarnation?"

Tony shivers. *I'm not
sure what I believe in,
Vanessa, other than there
has to be a better reason
for living than what I've
seen so far.*

Such an incredible waste
of energy, to work your ass
off for sixty years,
then shrivel up, die,
and be nothing more
than a memory—if you're
lucky enough to leave someone
behind who will *remember you.*
There must be more.
Don't you think?

Well, that conversation
took a sudden sharp turn.
I look him in the eye,
find total sincerity and a need
for someone to share his
universal questioning.
"Sure, Tony. I think
there's more.
I just wonder if
it's 'here'
or 'out there.'"

Speaking of Out There

Stanley has cornered
a short, zitty guy, who
he keeps calling "Flea."

> Paul moves in, yelling
> for Stanley to *shut the hell up
> and go sit this one out.*

Flea retreats to a corner
to smirk in Stanley's
direction, which stirs
everything up again.
Stanley stands, heads
in Flea's direction.

> Paul goes after Stanley,
> warning, *You're going to
> be sorry, shithead.*

> > Kate moves toward
> > Flea, warning, *If he
> > goes down, you go down.*

Tony pushes me back
toward the wall.
*This is going to be ugly.
Stay behind me.*

He's right, as Paul
wrestles Stanley down,
leveraging one fat body
with his own not-so-svelte one.

The room dissolves into howls
as Flea moves forward,
Ha-ha, asshole.

And Kate takes him
down, easy as pie.
What did I tell you?

I start to cry because
this place is insane, and if
I'm here, I must be insane too.
Tony turns, wraps his arms
around me. *Don't cry,
Vanessa. Everything's okay.
I'll always be here*

for you.

Conner

Now I Could Tell

A sordid tale of one
twin envying another,
of relentless competition,
even money on the win

until we were old enough
to learn the finer points
of cheating. You'd think
getting caught might concern

us. Not! Both of us had one
real goal in mind: attention,
especially from Dad, who seemed
to think his familial role

was demanding respect.
It's hard to respect someone
who outlines expectations
without regard to feasibility.

But I'm not going there,
so I'll try to placate
the bulldog. "Cara is bright,
I won't deny that. What I

don't understand is why
she feels the need to one-up
me, from clothes to stereos
to the finest wheels good

old Dad's money can buy. . . ."
Just as I decide maybe
there's more to the story
I'd like to confide after all,

>Dr. Starr's telephone rings.
>*One minute . . . uh-huh . . . oh!*
>*On my way. Sorry, Conner.*
>*Looks like we're done for the day.*

Dr. Starr Jumps Up

Almost overturns her big
armchair, moves swiftly
across to the door. Something
major has happened somewhere

in the building, that's for sure.
Who knew the bulldog could
move so fast? I wonder what
I should do—stay or follow?

> As if reading my mind, she
> demands, *Hurry up, Conner.*
> She sprints down the hall,
> pumping her hands forward

> and back. *Stay right behind*
> *me and don't interfere.*
> Then, to herself, *What were*
> *they thinking? This isn't TV!*

> *Dogs, cops, and takedowns—*
> *grandstanding! And tomorrow*
> *is visiting day. How many*
> *parents will be understanding?*

Dogs, cops, and takedowns?
And I missed all that, under
interrogation by Dr. Starr—
our weekly one-on-one tryst?

>   She swings a wide right toward
>   the dining hall, mutters
>   under her breath, *Damn if I'll*
>   *take the fall for this one.*

Not Again

This room is a setting
for lunacy. Paul and Kate
have a couple of guys down
on the floor. One is Stanley.

That dude is a walking
time bomb, always ready
to detonate, even when
his demeanor is calm.

So there he is, under Paul's
substantial knee. Little Kate
has proven she's more than
the mouse she appears to be.

And to my right, just inside
the door, Tony is holding
Vanessa like they're an item.
There's definitely more

to that relationship than
one might guess. As Dr. Starr
storms into the room, they pull
apart, press back against the wall.

I join them. "So, did you guys
get to see any of the action?
I was stuck in the confessional.
Can you tell me what happened?"

> *We're guessing it was a meth
> bust,* Tony says. *They hauled
> Todd out of here in handcuffs.
> The rest is just Stanley.*

We watch Dr. Bellows
and Dr. Starr extricate
Stanley from Paul's grasp.
Another bizarre day at

Aspen Springs.

Tony
Rumors Travel Fast

We hear from Justin,
          who heard from Dahlia,
who heard from who
          knows who, that Todd's
supplier was his brother,
          who stashed the meth

in a hollow-handled
          toothbrush. How this
deception was discovered
          will be debated for weeks.
"Probably a random pee
          test, don't you think?"

                    That, or his brother
                            got busted and turned
                    narc, Conner says.
                                    Vanessa has another
                                            theory. *Maybe guilt*
                                    got the best of him.

Conner and I just laugh.
        "Cranksters rarely feel
guilty about what they do.
        More likely, he felt proud
of himself—smug, even—
        for getting away with it."

                    Yeah, until the dog came
                            through the door, Conner
                    adds. *Then he probably*
                            felt like a total dumb shit.
                    Jeez, he'd already made
                            Level Three, hadn't he?

"Yes, and hey, guess what!
        I did too. Dr. Boston
told me yesterday."

                            Me too, says Vanessa.
                                    I hope that means
                            a trip out of here soon.

I Don't Tell Them

The one condition
        of my newly acquired
Level Three status—
        a successful interaction
with my father, who's
        coming to visit tomorrow.

To quit stressing over
        the thought, I ask,
"Do you have visitors coming?"

                        Vanessa answers, *My*
                                grandma will be here.
                        Can't wait to see her.

                Conner nods, stiff
                        as a mannequin. *My*
                mother has finally
                        agreed to come. I'd rather
                not see her, but have to,
                        to make Level Three.

"You haven't seen
        her yet? How long
have you been here?"

Six weeks, give or take.
            She hasn't even asked
to see me until now.

                    Vanessa snorts. *Sounds*
                            like your mom is almost
                    as wonderful as mine.

"Neither of them could
        be half as screwed
up as mine was," I say.

            We'll have to compare
                    notes one day, Conner
            says. *You in, Vanessa?*
                            Face the color of death,
                                    she replies, *Talking about*
                    Mama makes her real.

Major Insight

In only six words.
      "Well, someday
we'll swap stories."
      I offer Vanessa my most
engaging smile, and
      she tries to return it.

        Conner plays the game,
           plays it well. No need
to swap, really. I've
           got stories enough for
all of us. And if I include
           my dad, that will keep us

        entertained for hours.
           Oh, hey. Speaking of
entertainment, here
           come the fine doctors,
looking rather distressed.
           Suppose dinner will be late?

I'd say that's a given.
        Drs. Starr and Bellows
sweep across the room,
        faces red and chests
puffing. Bodies move
        to let them by, a wave

                of agitation. *All right,*
                        everyone, back to your
                rooms, commands Dr. Starr.
                Dinner will be a little
                late tonight, but I promise
                        you won't go hungry.

She's a regular sweetheart!
        People begin to shuffle
past, and as Vanessa
        moves to join them, I
reach for her hand.
        "Remember—you're not

alone."

Vanessa

Just Another Day

Trying to keep my head
above water—the azure water
I'm sliding down into now.
Too much confusion.
Too much upset.
Too much time
without a mood adjuster.
I'm sure I'm not
the only one, either.
The Pill Patrol better
put it in high gear.

Conner says he's been
here for six weeks,
which means I've been here
at least seven, maybe
closer to eight.
And I don't feel better.
Don't feel healed.
Don't feel clearer.
I could stay in a place
like this forever
and never get well.

You're not alone, Tony says,
and I believe
he believes that.

I'm here for you.
And I want to
believe that, too.

Don't cry, Vanessa.
But I can't
help crying now.

I Will Admit

Through flowing tears
that Tony has become
more than a friend to me.
He's a bright planet
in the dark morning
sky of my existence.
Somehow seeing him,
even with his varied flaws,
buoys me with hope.
I am better for knowing him.

Conner, too, although he's more
like a faraway star, brilliant,
but cold in his distance;
beautiful in his perfection,
but likely to burn too brightly,
snuff himself out.
I wonder where he came
from, what random joining
of energies created
such complexity.

*My mother finally asked
to see me*, Conner said,

and I wonder
what kind of
mother she is.

I'd rather not see her at
all, but have to. . . .

Now that I
can relate to
completely.

If I include stories about
my dad, we'll be entertained . . .

Stories about
Daddy are the stuff
movies are made of.

One Time He Came Home

For Christmas—an unusual
event in itself. We probably
saw him on holidays
two or three times over the years.
We worked and worked
to make the house beautiful
with paper chains, tinsel,
dollar-store candles, candy canes,
and a homemade gingerbread village.

Daddy arrived on Christmas Eve,
arms laden with presents—wrapped
in newspaper, cheered by colorful bows.
We wanted to open them right
then and there, but he made
us wait until morning,
                    because the best things
                    are worth waiting for.
We woke, filled with anticipation,
ran to the Christmas tree.
Daddy turned us around,
made us march down the hall
                    with respect for the meaning
                    of the day.

We sat on the floor, newspaper-
wrapped presents in our laps,
imagining all the wonderful
things inside. We opened them carefully,
peeling back layers of newsprint
until we reached the boxes,
sliced the Scotch tape with our fingernails,
lifted the flaps, and each of us found . . .

One MRE (Meal, Ready to Eat—
turkey, stuffing, and cranberry sauce,
in foil pouches); one Hershey bar;
and a handful of bullet casings,
                    because this is what
                    my men are getting today.
And one more thing: a scrap of paper
with a hand-scrawled
                    I love you,

                    Dad.

Conner

Tossing and Turning

Every lump in this mattress
a boulder against my back,
every wrinkle in the sheets
a two-by-four in my shoulder,

sleep denied by the fear
of what tomorrow's visit
will bring. I squeeze my eyes
shut, try to focus instead

on the events of today,
find some relief, conjuring
Vanessa's face. But then
visions of another face come,

black-and-white, frame by
frame, like in an old film noir.
Dark, my love for her was very
dark, a source of secret shame.

I get out of bed, go to
the window, look out on
a surreal scene—moonlight,
and in its muted glow, hints

of lacy flakes. Late March,
and snowing. Spring skiers
will be happy, but for me
it means a growing sense

of claustrophobia. To
sleep, I swallow Ativan.
Dr. B prescribed it when I
told her how nightmares keep

me awake. Every evening,
they bring me two. Usually,
I take one, stash the other.
Tonight I pray three will do.

A Voice Rouses Me

It's Kate, rattling my bars.
*Wake up, Sykes. It's almost
eight and you missed breakfast.
Dr. Starr will give you a break*

*this time, mostly because
your parents are coming
today. Usually, missing
a meal will score you a*

*level drop. I know you
don't want that, so haul
your ass out of bed.* Her
arrogant tone is a taunt.

I rouse myself, try to
clear the Ativan fog,
lifting inside my head,
leaving fear in its place.

Dreams I cannot remember
have stirred another part of
me. I decide to let Kate see.
Without a word, I toss back

the blankets and climb from
bed, pajamas pointing stiffly
in Kate's direction. She just
smiles. *Was it something I said?*

Your parents arrive at nine.
I suggest you get rid of that,
one way or another, then get
dressed in something decent.

No problem. I need neither
palm nor cold shower to
shrivel me instantly.
My mom is on her way.

Nine A.M. Exactly

I knock on Dr. Starr's door.
Voices inside fade to black.
Despite the rumpled Lauren,
I reach for some semblance of pride.

> *Come in, Conner,* calls Dr.
> Starr, but my slippery hand
> fumbles the knob and it's
> Dad, on the far side of the door,

>> who opens it, pulling me
>> through and right up against
>> him. It's the closest we've ever
>> been, two strangers touching.

>> Immediately, he comes to
>> his senses, jerks backward.
>> *H-hello, son. Good to see you.*
>> Every muscle tenses, as if

I might try to hug him or
something perverse like that.
"Hello, Dad," I answer, also
shifting into a quick reverse.

*Will you please come inside and
close the door?* Mom gives me
a cold once-over. *I see you haven't
learned to care for your clothes.*

My face ignites and words
steam from my mouth before
I can stop them. "And I see
you're still a supreme bitch."

She doesn't even blink. *Even
a female dog wants her puppies
clean and wrinkle-free—unless,
of course, she's a Shar Pei.*

Touché.

Tony
Breakfast Is Cold

Well, okay, the eggs
            are almost lukewarm,
but the butterlike
            substance won't melt
on the toast. Everything
            gags me, trying to go down.

The mood is cool, too.
            Too much excitement
yesterday plus a late
            med delivery. If everyone
else feels like me, we
            all want to go back to bed.

And then, of course,
            we have visiting day
to deal with. I guess
            a few of these freakazoids
might like seeing their
            families come Saturday.

But my hunch is most
　　　　of them find themselves
here because of the scene
　　　　back home. Someone
had to check them in—
　　　　like who would volunteer?

Across the room, Vanessa
　　　　picks at her eggs, like she's
looking for bugs. She's
　　　　sitting alone, like she always
does. Funny, 'cause most
　　　　of the girls buddy up like hens.

I wonder what pain she's
　　　　got bottled up inside, what
secrets she refuses to tell.
　　　　I wonder if making her
mother "real" is the only
　　　　thing she's afraid of.

I've Got My Own

Fears to face in a few
       minutes, the main one
being I'll blow it again.
       I didn't even realize how
pissed I was at my dad
       until we were three feet apart.

              Anthony, boy, you got
                    the Ceccarelli temper,
              Ma always used to say.
                    Be careful, or it will
              burn you out early,
                    just like your father.

One of the few things
       I do remember about
him, in fact, was his
       temper. He'd come
home to Ma's less-than-
       mediocre housekeeping,

throw down his briefcase.
Emma? Turn off the TV
and get your ass out
here. What exactly
do you do all day,
besides soap operas?

That was when he thought
soap operas was all she did.
I knew about her playing
around years before he did.
Came home from school
more than once to hear

bedsprings squeaking,
disgusting human noises.
Once or twice I got brave
enough to crack the door
and peek inside to see
what no kid ever should.

But That's a Different Story

Than the one I'm going
       to tell now, with Dr. Boston
mediating this time.
            Please come in, Tony,
                she says. *Sit right over*
            there, next to your father.

He doesn't stand this
       time, the "no hug" rule
in effect. "Hello, Dad."
                  Hello, Anthony. First,
                    I want to apologize for
                the last time I was here.

I shrug. "No worries.
       We both have some
things to work through."
            That's why we're here,
                chirps the Widow. *Let's*
            start with you, Tony.

            Can you tell us, in one
                sentence, why you're so
            angry at your father?

One sentence, to sum
        up years of resentment?
I will not cry! Will not!

"Because he chose not
        to be part of my life, not even
when I needed him the most."
                Fair enough. Can you
                        respond to that in one
                sentence, Mr. Ceccarelli?

                        Dad thinks a second.
                                I stayed away because I
                        couldn't stomach the guilt.

Communication.

Vanessa

Breakfast Is Lousy

But even if it were perfect,
I couldn't taste a thing.
I'm neither up nor down
today, just cruising in shades
of gray—a cold, colorless
place, something like
being dead, I guess.
Maybe I am dead
and just don't know it yet.

Some people say ghosts
don't know they're dead,
so they keep moving
through the same old
buildings, the same old
streets, trying to talk
to people there, to find
out why they can waltz
through plaster walls
like they're water.
I think that would give
me a pretty good clue.
Far as I know, I can't
pass through a wall.
Think I should try?

Enough, already. I add
my plate to the "scrape
and rinse" stack, almost
wishing they would give
me kitchen duty—unlikely,
considering my passion
for sharp instruments.
But it would give me something
to concentrate on besides
seeing Grandma in an hour
or so. It makes her so sad
to visit me here.
And that makes me sad.
Sad, and cruising gray.

I Go Back to My Room

Think about trying
to walk through the wall,
opt for the door instead;
dig through my drawers
for my favorite denim
skirt and a light blue cotton
blouse, long-sleeved;
lay them out on the bed,
as if I were in them.
Before I change, there's
something I have to do.

The bandage is long gone
from my left hand, and my fingers
almost work right again.
There's a pretty scar,
like little knots, joining
hand to arm. If I cut there,
I'll ruin the artwork.
I look at my right wrist,
wearing a bracelet
of little scabs. Can't cut
there. Someone will see.
Through the gray haze,
a cloud of frustration rises.

But I've got a new secret
weapon. Yesterday, when
all was in chaos, I noticed
an empty Coke can in a wastepaper
basket. No one
observed as I reached
down, extracted the pull top.
I remove it from its hiding
place beneath my dresser.
Run one finger lightly
over its lovely saw-
toothed edge. Place
it on the fold line inside
my left elbow. Close my
eyes and let it bite. Easy
now, a shallow cut is all
I need to slice through the gray.

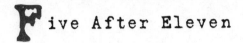

Five After Eleven

I walk into Dr. Starr's office,
dressed in the clean denim skirt
and blue cotton blouse,
smiling at the deception,
wrapped in toilet paper,
hidden beneath long sleeves.

Grandma comes over,
gives me a hug, and I
hope she doesn't wonder
why I don't hug back
with much enthusiasm.
You look so pretty today,
Vanessa. Blue suits you.

Dr. Starr interrupts the syrupy
stuff. *Your grandmother*
and I have been talking,
Vanessa. Please have a seat.
Now, why haven't you
told me about your mother?

I feel the smile slip from
my face but don't know
exactly how to respond.
"Wh-what about her,
exactly?" I bend my left
arm, squeeze tightly, wince
at the beautiful pain.

> *You never mentioned*
> *her BPD. Bipolar disorder*
> *happens to be genetic.*
> *Did you know that?*
> She waits for me to nod.
> *It's also very treatable.*
> *So why haven't you*
> *said anything?*

I smile at the throb
in the crook of my
left arm. "You never

asked."

Conner

Postcards from Home

That's what my parents' visit
reminded me of. Dad talked
about my straight-A status,
my goal of a law degree.

> *He must maintain his GPA,*
> agreed Mom. *I expect you'll*
> *see to it, Dr. Starr. I feel*
> *the need to underline that.*

> That was funny—Mom
> made the bulldog blink.
> *That will be up to Conner,*
> *I'm afraid, Mrs. Sykes.*

Dad talked about sports.
He's a star running back.
I hope this experience
won't bar him from playing.

> *Conner will have to remain*
> *on medication for some*
> *time. His coach will drug-test—*
> *that's a foregone conclusion.*

And that made Mom blink.
*Medication? What do you
mean? Surely you have no
expectation we'll allow*

*him to use drugs? That
goes against everything
we stand for as parents.
Who knows how he'd end up?*

> Dr. Starr cleared her throat.
> *Conner is suffering from
> severe depression. Prescription
> medication is his best hope.*

Did They Even Know

I was in the room? Did
they care? "Hello, everyone.
Conner to Earth. Are any
of you even aware

that I'm sitting right here?
Quit talking about me like
I don't belong in this
conversation. Don't you get

that in the space of just
a few months I'll be all
by myself, out on my own,
and none of you will matter?"

Well spoken, if maybe
a bit blunt. But it wasn't
a touchdown. More like
an ineffectual punt.

Mom picked up the ball at
a hard sprint. *I just don't
understand how you could
treat us with so little regard.*

We have standing in this
community, a reputation
to protect. Did you expect
to act with impunity?

"I'm sure you can't understand
this, Mom, but everything
isn't about you." I looked her
in the eye, willed myself calm.

"What I did had nothing to do
with you. It was about letting
myself feel—desire, pain, fear.
Emotions you don't permit."

Totally Straightforward

In fact, maybe as honest
as I've ever been, but did
they get it? No frigging way.
They'll never understand.

At least the bulldog was cool.
Let's all relax, shall we?
Assigning blame and laying
guilt won't change the facts.

Conner seems to be doing
well. He has opened up
in therapy and I believe
he will excel in the classroom.

What we need to work on
now is the family dynamic.
But without your cooperation,
I don't see how that's possible.

Mom reacted about as
expected. *We're here, aren't*
we? Don't you dare say that we have
neglected to cooperate.

> *What I mean, Mrs. Sykes,*
> *is that we must tone down*
> *the rhetoric. It's the only*
> *way to mitigate confrontation.*

No more, no less, time was up.
Dad reached for my hand, shook
it good-bye, just like a client.
I'm glad you're making progress.

Mom refused to look at me,
so I took the high road. "Bye,
Mom." And as I turned to
go, Dr. Starr said,   "Conner? Level

Three."

Tony

Guess My Level Three Status

Is safe for now. It
        was good to hear
from Dad's lips that he
        took some blame
for the things that have
        happened in my life.

        God knows there's
            enough blame to go
        around, Anthony,
            he said. But it breaks
        my heart to know
            that maybe I could

        have made things
            easier, saved you
        pain. I had it all
            wrong last time,
        Anthony, when I said
            I could forgive you.

See, I asked the Man
            Upstairs for forgiveness.
He told me I had to
            ask you first. Forgive
me, son, for not
            being a father to you.

It was like he dropped
            a half ton of bricks,
straight into my belly.
            If God really had something
to do with this, how
            could I say no? On the other

hand, how could I be
            sure, 1. God *did* have
something to do with
            it and, 2. Dad *really*
meant what he said?
            "I need to think it over."

We Left It at That

Better than how we
          left things last time,
for sure. I even let
          him give me a hug
good-bye. It felt really
          weird, uncomfortable

for both of us. I think
          I even held my breath,
and when he let go, I
          felt numb, like he'd squeezed
me too hard. Three
          hours later I'm still numb.

I don't know if I can
          step forward, let go
of a decade of hard
          feelings, even if God
does want me to.
          It's a damn hard test.

Part of me says, *What*
         the hell, give him a chance.
It's not so much to ask.
         Another part screams,
Another chance to what?
         Screw you over again?

This totally sucks. I mean
         I've been given something
I dreamed about for too
         many years—the chance
to know my father again.
         So why can't I embrace him?

Things were so much
         easier when I was just
Tony, who nobody
         cared about. Maybe
not better, but for real—
         a whole lot simpler.

Think I'll Wander

Down to the rec room.
>> See who else has been
shredded today.
>>>> Carmella waves as I
>>> walk through the door.
>>> *Hey, Tony. What's shaking?*

"Nothing can shake
>> quite like you, dear.
Love your blouse."
>>> She glances down at
>>>> the flawless turquoise
>>> silk. *This ol' thing? Thanks!*

Carmella is great—a
>> part-time house mother
at age twenty-three.
>> My hunch is she won't
last long. She cares
>> much too much about us.

In fact, from what
         I've heard, the burnout
rate for staff at places
         like this is exactly
three years. Seems
         optimistic to me.

I can't even imagine
         dealing with a bunch
of emotional cripples,
         not to mention a few
total wackos, day in,
         day out, for three years.

                         And so, Tony, calls sweet
                                 Carmella, *come here,*
                         tell me about your day.
Why not? Who knows?
         Maybe she's got a
personal line to the Man

Upstairs.

Vanessa

The Cat's Out of the Bag

Grandma told Dr. Starr
all about Mama's gear
shifting, and how she
ended up—minus my
relatively major part
in the soap opera, of course.
Glad Grandma doesn't
know all my secrets.

> *Vanessa is very protective
> of her mother,* Grandma
> said. *She doesn't often
> share information of
> such a sensitive nature.
> None of us do, in fact.
> Her father would have
> a conniption fit.*

> *I can understand wanting
> to protect her privacy,*
> said Dr. Starr. *And I can
> understand your wanting
> to protect your granddaughter.*

However, we cannot make real progress unless we put everything out in the open, so we know exactly what we're dealing with.

So now I will start a new
regimen of treatment.
Lithium, here I come,
weight gain, runs, and all.
But hey, I didn't break
down and confess.
Grandma turned
traitor, not me.
God love her.

And Through It All

No one noticed how
I kept my arm bent tight.
Good thing, too.
A thin, red line stains
my pretty blue blouse,
right at the crease
in the elbow. Guess
I cut a little deeper
than I meant to.
Better be careful.
I'd hate for my arm
to drop off at dinner
or something. Ha.

A cold-water rinse
is called for, but I'd better
wait until later tonight,
when everyone's back
in their rooms and the bathroom
offers more privacy.

Meanwhile, I change
back into my sweats,
Saturday red, same
as all the other Aspen
Springs residents. Identity
isn't something they
encourage here.

My shirt is barely over
my head, pants still
on the bed, when the door
opens suddenly.
It's Paul, with goodies.

                        His eyes immediately fall
                        to the V between my legs.
                        Sorry for barging in, but
                        Dr. Starr wants you to start
                        on the lithium right away.
                        Take this, then finish getting

                        dressed.

Conner

Nothing's Different

Level Three. Awesome,
movies, mall trips, maybe
a barbecue in the park—
small perks for facing up

to Mom. Holy crap. I'd
almost forgotten just what
a bitch that woman can
be, a rotten example

of humanity. Wonder
if she has any, stashed
inside. And Dad? He was
only civil to free himself

of the nagging thought
that he might somehow be
responsible for the things
I've done. Quite likely, Dad.

His parting remark as I
closed the door was so
Dad-like. *Be sure to keep
an eye on your GPA.*

Still carping about my
grades, hoping I'll land
a scholarship so he won't
have to worry about coping

with an Ivy League tuition.
A state university won't
do for dear old Dad. No,
that's a fate worse than death.

Wonder how he would have
felt if I'd done the deed
correctly. I wonder if he
or Mom would even have cried.

Another Level Three Perk

Is holidays at home, but
I don't care about going
home for Easter or Fourth
of July. It was a rare

occasion for us to
celebrate holidays
together, and certainly
not without debate over

stupid things like turkey
or ham; fireworks in Reno,
Tahoe, or Virginia City.
Damn if I'll miss any of that.

July. Will I still be in this
place then? Would I rather
be home, biding time in
a state of total disgrace?

Would they leave me alone
long enough to call Emily?
Would she take my call? Could
I be strong if she didn't?

Would she even be home?
Or maybe she's moved away
from her husband, her students,
the hound dog press. And me.

How much does everyone
at school know? Stupid question.
The best-rehearsed denials
can't fool inquiring minds.

My first day back will be hell—
the debris of my many
failures. I wonder how
a GED affects GPA.

None of It

Has much affected my
appetite. Dinner, I hear,
is served, and I plan to eat
every carb and fat-laden bite.

Why worry about calories,
spare tires, lethargy? Living
medicated allows me
not to care. Anyway,

Level Three also affords
me the chance to exercise.
Lifting until I ache or
jogging myself into a trance

are the best ways I can
think of to forget about
the big picture. Straddling
the brink of exhaustion,

blood thumping in my ears.
Clawing air, the only thing
worth worrying about,
drawing another breath.

The very idea makes me high.
God, I sound like a bipolar
lunatic. Pack 'em on, pound
'em off. I could cry, because

either way, it doesn't matter.
Dinner table, here I come,
salivating at the spaghetti
and meatball perfume.

Tony waves me over. Hell,
why not? We can trade tales.
Hope his are as juicy as
the ones I've got. Downright

messy.

Tony

Spaghetti and Meat Blobs

Not even sure about
          the "meat" part,
although they kind
          of taste like dog
food. Okay, like
          dog food smells.

I won't admit to
          eating it, not out
loud. Surprising,
          the crap you'll eat
if you get hungry
          enough. Worse crap

than this, even, and this
          is pretty damn bad—
Meatball-like Crap
          in a Can. Served
lukewarm over half-
          cooked spaghetti.

Jeez, Conner is sure
        loading up his plate.
I can't believe anyone
        would want a double
helping of *this*. "Hey
        Conner, come here."

                        He sits across from me,
                                grinning like Alice's
                        goofball cat. *What's up?*

I point to his plate. "Not
        much. I just thought you
might want mine, too."

                        Not sure I want this.
                                I was starving until I
                        got an up-close look.

We Decide

All the parents must
          have finished their
visiting early and
          gone home long before
the kitchen got busy
          reinventing dog food.

                    I don't know if my
                              parents would have
                    been more horrified
                              or satisfied. Conner
                    laughs. *My mom would*
                              probably have puked.

"We all may puke before
          the evening is over. Damn,
can you see it? Marinara
          and meat by-products,
splashed across stalls
          and walls. Yeah, man!"

Conner wrinkles his nose.
*Well, I'm gonna chance
it. My stomach is turning
cartwheels. Catharsis
makes for a healthy
appetite, I guess.*

"Catharsis, eh? Sounds
like you had an interesting
day. Want to cough up
a few details?" Of
course, turnabout's
fair play. I don't mind.

Sure, he says, around
a big, smooshy bite.
*Just give me a few
minutes to choke
down this delicious
Chef Boyar-Don't meal.*

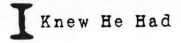
I Knew He Had

A wicked sense
            of sarcasm—Conner's
brand of humor. Mine
            too, tell the truth.
Maybe that's why I
            like the guy. No one

could be as straight-
            arrow as the person
he lets the world see.
            Totally plugged up.
That's how most people
            would describe him.

But there's a kernel
            there . . . something
worth trying to grow.
            Don't ask me what.
Might be worth trying
            to figure it out.

He's giving the rundown
          on visiting day.
Dr. Starr gave me Level
          Three, mostly I think
because I held my tongue
          but still held my ground.

Dad, at least, tried to
          pretend he gave half
a damn. Yeah, right.
          Mom will always
be the total uptight
          c-u-you know what.

Interesting, that he
          doesn't just say
the word. Some sort
          of psychology there.
Sheesh, who's the therapist
          around here,

anyway?

Vanessa

It's the First Time

I've faced this situation.
I feel violated. Raped
by Paul's eyes. I hold out
my hand and he drops
my new salvation into my
outstretched palm, eyes
barely lifting as he says,

It will take a few weeks
to really feel the effects,
so don't panic if your mood
swings intensify for a while.
We'll keep you on the Prozac,
too, just in case.

Oh, great. Fixed and ruined
at the same time. Oh, well.
They're the experts.
Like I really believe that.

Dinner is everyone's favorite,
spaghetti à la Aspen Springs.
Hurry up. Wouldn't want
to miss out, would you?

He backs away, eyes still
on a point somewhere around
three feet off the ground.
"Thanks, Paul," I say,
turning my back to him.
Not that I'm not positive
he's scoping out my butt
in exactly the same way.
The door closes and I rush
to slide on my pants before
he decides he's forgotten
to tell me something.
Then I take aim
at the dining room.

I Guess You Could

Call this mess of red starch
spaghetti. Most of the girls
around me don't seem to care,
gulping it down like chocolate.
Or maybe like something else.

Check out my face, says
Dahlia. *What does it look
like I've been scarfing?*
Her grin is ringed a messy,
wet scarlet.

*You probably would,
too*, answers Devon.
*Personally, I'd wait
at least a week.*

Gack! Disgusting. What
is it with these people?
Thank goodness they don't
seem inclined to include
me in their sick banter.

Just to prove me wrong,
Dahlia asks loudly,
What about you, Vanessa?
You ever munch carpet?

I consider the best way
to answer such a loaded,
leading question. My usual
way of dealing with such
things is withdrawal. Tonight,
something wicked comes
over me. "Never have, dear.
Maybe because the first one
I ever saw looked so much
like yours. Scared me to death."

The Table Busts Up

Dahlia's face flares.
You sucking bitch.

This is kind of fun.
"No, sweetie, I just told
you I don't lean your
direction. Of course, from
what I hear, you teeter-
totter. Is that true?"

Her mouth drops and she
stares at my face, no doubt
trying to figure out just what
has come over me. Confusion
ping-pongs in her eyes.
Wh-who told you that?

This is really fun. Can
it be the lithium, despite
Paul's prediction? I don't
think so, so it must be
a bloom of mania. I'm a long,
long way above blue.

"Why, everyone. Don't
you know about the room-
to-room gossip chain?
'Trade you two mediocre
rumors for one really
good one about Dahlia.'"

She could go either way.
Perhaps thankfully, she chooses
the easy way. *Ha! Who turned
you on, anyway, Vanessa?
You're pretty funny
once you get going.
Who knew you even
had a sense of*

humor?

Conner

The Girls' Side of the Room

Jacks up with laughter, and
it looks like lovely Vanessa
is involved. Dahlia resembles
a cobra, ready to strike,

given just a bit more
provocation. I wonder
what Vanessa said, and
what was her motivation

to poke a verbal stick
at such a reactive serpent.
Her willingness to parry
makes her even more attractive.

> *How fun*, comments Tony.
> *I think we're seeing a whole
> other side of Vanessa. Who'd
> have guessed she could cause a stink?*

"All women have an evil
side. One minute they've got
their tongue down your throat,
the next they slice you wide open."

I don't have much experience
with the fair sex, but the ones
I have known have never given
me much trouble. I swear, they

are much better friends than men.
Of course, most men either
avoid me like the plague, or
swear their undying love.

I smile. "Don't look at me.
Love is for children and
dimwads." Most of me felt
that way long before Emily.

But I Am Curious

"So . . . have you ever slept
with a woman—tried a walk
on the 'other side'? I mean,
have you always been gay?"

I expect him to tell me what
most gay guys say—that it's
not a matter of choice,
that they were born that way.

But he doesn't say anything,
not right away. His face goes
blank while he thinks about
the right way to answer.

> *I've never slept with a girl,*
> *but I never really had*
> *the chance. I've spent a lot*
> *of time in lockup. I try*
>
> *to believe that I was born*
> *gay. But I'm not really*
> *sure that's true. When I was*
> *eight, this piece-of-slime boyfriend*

*of my ma's asked me to come
back into the bedroom to see
"something special." You can
guess what he wanted to do.*

*The only thing I knew about
sex before that was it made my
ma scream. That day I screamed
too. Ma chose to ignore it.*

*Later she said it was all
my fault because I—no doubt
something genetic from my
dad's side—was a little faggot.*

*Not long after, I was confined
with boys, looking to act like
men. And there were a few guards
who used us for their sex toys.*

Way Too Much Information

But hey, I asked, didn't I?
I don't know what to say,
what to do. Instinct tells me
to reach out and touch him, but no

way. The other guys might get
the wrong impression. *Tony*
might get the wrong impression.
Suddenly I have a strong

urge to move to another
table. What I don't understand
is how, despite the lurid tales
he recited, Tony seems so stable.

Hey, sorry, man. Didn't
mean to unload. Not looking
for sympathy. Hope what I
just told you stays between

you and me. I haven't
even owned up to all that
in therapy. Guess I've never
been quite stoned enough.

"No problem, bro. Who
would I tell, even if it was
important?" And it's not.
What the hell? The best thing

about our conversation
is the realization that others
have problems as big as—or bigger
than—my own. Mine are huge. His

are insurmountable.

Tony

What Got into Me?

Like Conner needed—
            or wanted—to know
any of that garbage.
            Jeez, fire me up, it's
hard to put me out.
            At least he didn't look

too put off by what
            I said. Wonder what
he'd think if I confessed
            the rest. I haven't
told anyone since
            I spilled to Phillip.

                    Conner almost gives
                            me no choice. *So what
                    did you do, man?*
                            *I mean, why did they
                    lock you up? And how
                            long were you in for?*

Should I go ahead
            and tell him? It
might make him
            freak out completely.
And I kind of like
            having his company.

I'm sick of holding it
            inside, sick of it escaping
my head every night when
            I dream. Thank God for
Aspen Springs sleeping aids.
            I don't remember my dreams.

I decide to compromise.
            "I was in for aggravated
assault on my ma's jerk-off
            boyfriend. I spent six
mother-humping years,
            beating meat in juvie."

Conner's Sympathetic

Six years? For that?
                    he asks, eyes flashing
anger. *The asshole*
                    deserved it. Did you
happen to get your mom,
                    too? She deserved more.

"Why didn't I think
          of that?" It's a joke.
I definitely thought
          about it—I had lots
of spare time to create
          great revenge fantasies.

Still, "But she got hers
          anyway. It wasn't the next
boyfriend, or the one
          after, or the one after that.
But one of them nailed
          her, first with his fists,

then with a hammer.
        It wasn't too long
after they let me out,
        maybe a year. By
then, I'd emancipated
        myself. No one missed me."

                    Shit, man, you were
                            right. Your mom
                    may have been even
                            more screwed up
                    than mine. Hard to
                            believe that's possible.

Maybe I will tell him
        the rest after all. But
not tonight. I've tested
        the water—calm water.
Telling the rest will be
        like testing a tsunami.

Think I'll Skip

"Recreating" tonight.
        My head is too full
of too many bad
        memories. On my
way back to my
        room, I find Paul,

letting spaghetti
        junk clog in my
throat. I manufacture
        a loogie, hawk
it into a napkin.
        "Hey, dude," I say,

"I think I'm coming
        down with a cold.
Can you bring me
        something for it?"
Sudafed and Halcyon
        (my regular sleep helper

in this place) should
        put me far beyond
the reach of nightmares.

Have to clear it first,
            Paul says. *Give me*
a couple of minutes.

It doesn't take long.
        In fact, I doubt he
cleared it with anyone,
        but who cares? He
pretended to do his
        duty anyway.

I gag down a big
        spoon of the sticky
red syrup, chase it
        with a little white pill,
lay down on the bed,
        and wait for my head

to drift.

Vanessa

TV Tonight

Was a rerun of *Fear Factor*.
Every juvenile space cadet
really should watch six
adult space cadets, jumping
off buildings and eating
mouse entrails. Mmmm.
Looked just like the spaghetti.

What was Carmella thinking?
She's such a ditz, but at
least she bothers to relate,
unlike the other house
mothers—Linda, a hard
little woman of forty or so,
and Arlene, who must
be pushing seventy.

Linda is all business—yes,
no, shut the hell up—and
totally capable of a takedown.
Arlene lives in her own
oddball world, one she
dreamed up before my
parents were born.

Guess she can't make
it on Social Security.
But working here?
She must be as crazy
as the rest of us.

I sit at the window,
staring into the darkness,
waiting for everything
to fall completely quiet
before making a bathroom
run. The inside of my
head feels like a blender,
whirling a strange
concoction of this
morning's Prozac
and this evening's lithium.

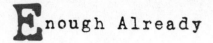

Enough Already

I really do need
to use the bathroom—
a likely side effect
from the blended mess
in my brain. And how
will I ever sleep tonight?

One problem at a time.
I reach under my mattress,
extract the blouse,
stained red at the elbow,
stash it under my sweats.
Then I open the door,
poke my head into
the hall. "May I go to
the bathroom, please?"

No answer. Unusual.
Someone is always
monitoring the cameras
in the corridors. I decide
to go anyway, plead
diarrhea if I'm caught.

The girls' bathroom
is five doors down,
on the left. You have
to ask for permission
to go because once you're
inside, they kind of have
to give you some privacy,
at least in the stalls.

I go on in, turn on the cold
water, and as I start
to rinse my sleeve,
I notice I'm
not alone.

One Stall, Four Feet

That's what the mirror
reveals, and a volley
of *shush*es at the sound
of water in the sink.
One pair of feet quickly
lifts, and as I watch,
it comes to me the shoes
look awfully large
to belong to a girl.
That, and the soles
are facing out, heels up.

I make a big deal of
drying my hands, loudly
wadding the paper towels
and tossing them in the trash.
Then I go to the door, open
and shut it without exiting.

> *Quick! You're squashing
> me.* Dahlia's voice.
> > *Just a minute. I'm
> > not finished.* Paul's.
> *Well, hurry up. We're
> gonna get busted.*

Whoever that was
shouldn't have been
here. She didn't
get permission.
So what are you going
to do? Bust her?

No wonder no one
was manning the cameras.
Paul was manning Dahlia.
Ugh. I make a quick escape
before he *does* finish.
And only when I'm back
in my room do I remember
that I really do have to go
to the bathroom. Like, right

now.

Conner

Today We Have a Visitor

In the classroom. I get there
a few minutes before nine,
overhear her conversing with
Mr. Hidalgo, who whispers

behind the half-closed door. *These
kids are the best of the worst—
bright, capable underachievers.
It's truly bizarre*

*that they end up here. For
some it's addiction, for
others, abuse. A few simply
succumb to depression.*

The others arrive. We push
inside. It's the perfect chance
to rub up against Vanessa, one
I decide to take advantage of.

Nice, how the top of her head
nests perfectly under my chin.
I want to let my hands circle
her waist, lift to her small breasts.

Something stirs, for the first
time in weeks, and it has
nothing to do with Emily—
or a taste for expert sin.

Vanessa can't help but
react. *Unusual way
to say hello, Conner.
Rather overt, in fact.*

But she doesn't pull away,
or move my hand from the curve
of her back. And both of us
understand the meaning of that.

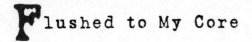Flushed to My Core

I walk stiffly to my seat.
Stiff, yeah, that's it, okay.
Three rows over, Vanessa
smiles, and I wonder if

she's feeling a little "stiff"
too. No time to think about
it now. Mr. Hidalgo clears
his throat, ready to do his thing.

> *We have someone special*
> *here today. Ms. Littell is*
> *an artist-in-residence,*
> *and we're going to hear*
>
> *from her all about how to*
> *write great poetry. No groans.*
> *I'm sure you all have what it*
> *takes to create a poem.*

Ms. Littell draws herself
up real straight. Teaching
us posture, too? Or trying
to feel more in control?

She talks about herself
for ten minutes—who she is,
what she does, how well
published she is. Then she

rambles on for another
half hour about what makes
a poem good—word choice,
the power of metaphor.

Finally she instructs,
Write a poem about your
happiest memory.
Excite me with your words.

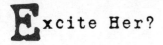Excite Her?

Was she talking to me?
Not if she expects that to
happen over my happiest
memory, whatever that

might be. I sit, dissecting
my childhood, think about
holidays and vacations,
most of them good enough

if you measure by toys,
clothes, cool things to do, but
can *things* really make you
happy? I suppose some

people think so. I remember
one time spending a week
with a friend. His family
didn't have much. Except fun.

The concept stunned me. Fun, with
his mom and dad? Fun, with
his sister? He even had fun
with his grandparents. Mine bore

me to death—the two that are
still alive, anyway. Dad's
parents died before I was born,
left him a mint in their will.

Ms. Littell stands, hands on
hips, waiting for me to write
something. I'm sure that she's
anticipating something else.

I put my pen to paper,
begin: *My happiest memories*
are sun-streaked afternoons
in the cinnamon arms of

my Emily. . . .

Tony

What Is It

With these artsy types?
        Happy memories? Excite
her with my words?
        Does she have half
a clue what kind of
        kids she's dealing with?

If we were wallowing
        in happy memories,
would we be here at all?
        I can't remember a single
group session dedicated
        to happiness; not one

conversation about
        the Magic Kingdom
called Home. Now
        Nathan might believe
there's a Magic Kingdom
        in some distant galaxy,

and maybe he's happy,
       letting his mind—what
there is of it—wander
       to that place. And no
doubt Justin smiles when
       he goes to bed at night,

chants a mantra to his
       Lord, prays for quick
deliverance. I guess
       he might be happy
in his dreams, rocking
       in the arms of seraphim.

But then I look at
       Conner, frustrated
with his memories,
       and Vanessa, who
stares at the table,
       longing for her knife.

I'm Pretty Sure

She knows that Conner
            and I know. What I
don't get at all is that
            no one else seems to
have noticed the way
            she hides the blood.

Maybe she'll write
            her poem about how
happy it makes her
            feel to ease her skin
open, drown herself
            in the ebb of tide

within her veins. Damn
            if that's not poetic.
Maybe I should write
            that, here on this
blank, white piece
            of paper. Blank

as the slate in my
             brain that is supposed
to have happy
             memories etched
on its clean, shiny
             surface. All I find is black.

I close my eyes, assess
             my life, search for
a scene worth reliving.
             The first thing that comes
to mind is the day I
             got out of lockup, free

to walk wherever I chose,
             talk to whoever happened
by, without having to ask
             permission. And then
it came to me that I had
             only one place to go.

My Ma Picked Me Up

Apparently, like it or
         not, it was a parent's
duty to sign a kid out.

> *Ready to go? Ha-ha!*
>   *Stupid question. Would*
> *you get a move on?*

Apparently, she had
         better things to do
than catch up with me.

> *You sure are scrawny.*
>   *Didn't they feed you three*
> *squares in that place?*

Apparently, she was
         worried that she might
have to fatten me up.

> *I'm living in a new*
>   *place—a studio.*
> *Have a new man, too.*

Apparently, she thought
         I gave a fuck about who
she was sleeping with.

Watch out for Pete. He's
    got a temper, 'specially
when he's drinking.

Apparently she believed
    I would let another one
of her lousy boyfriends
    abuse me—in whatever
ways. Wasn't going
    to happen. Not ever again.

I followed her up two
    flights of stairs at a fleabag
weekly motel. Took
    one look at the "studio" I
was supposed to share
    with Ma and Pete. Hit

the streets.

Vanessa

Prozac, Lithium, and Conner

One, two, or all of them
have put me in a completely
happy space. Can I write
about now—this instant?
Pencil to paper, in perfect
round cursive, I begin:

Memory is a tenuous thing. . . .

(I know, I've lately
said that, but it's true.)

*flickering glimpses, blue
and white, like ancient,
decomposing 16mm film.
Happiness escapes
me there, where faces
are vague and yesterday
seems to come tied
up in ribbons of pain.*

(There must be
happiness there
somewhere, but
I can't find it.)

Happiness? I look for it instead
in today, where memory
is something I can still
touch, still rely on.
I find it in the smiles
of new friends, the hope
blossoming inside.

(Scary, but accurate.)

My happiest memories
have no place in the
past; they are those
I have yet to create.

Those I Have Yet to Create

That must mean I plan
to create them. Funny,
when I got here, coasting
through life was the best
I figured I'd ever do—
managing the seesaw
with substances
or the slice of a blade.

So much blue
in my days, a spattering
of white, an abstract of
emotions, painting every
choice I ever made, hope
rarely represented
on that deviant canvas.
But here it is, a hint
of bronze, a shimmer
of gold frost.

Can my world fill
with color? Will I ever
live shades of red?
Yellow? Green?

When I think of Mama,
it all goes blue; memories
of Trevor are rooted in white.

Conner's hand at my back,
and the surge of his masculinity
at the tip of my tailbone,
made me shiver copper.
I don't know what
that means.
I only know
I liked it.

Suddenly, My Hands

Begin to shake, just a little
at first, then building,
building, tremoring,
an earthquake.
My pencil falls to the floor
with a loud clatter
and everyone turns to stare.
I bend to retrieve it,
but my hand refuses
to go where my brain
tries to point it.

> *Vanessa? Are you
> all right?* Mr. Hidalgo
> jumps from his chair,
> reaches my side almost
> as quickly as Tony.

> *Vanessa? What's wrong?*
> Tony's eyes, frightened,
> tell me I look even
> worse than I feel.

> *Vanessa?* Conner
> joins the party.
> *Let me help you.*

The three of them, all
talking at once, make
my brain hurt, trying
to keep up, churn it
into dizziness. And that
makes me want to throw
up. I feel the blood rush
from my face and jump
to my feet. "I have to go
to the bathroom."

No one tries to stop me,
which is a very good thing.
I burst through the door,
into a stall, lean over the bowl,

let fly.

Conner

Ms. Littell Looks Horrified

Oh, the poor thing, she says.
Hope it wasn't my assignment.
She leans over Vanessa's
desk, decides to sit, reads

the neatly scripted words.
This is beautiful, she tells
the entire room. *I wonder
if Ms. O'Reilly would mind*

if I shared her poem. So
she does, and it is more
than beautiful—it lets us
see the inside of Vanessa.

She's looking for happiness
in today, and some unknown
part of me—some stranger—
wants to give some joy away.

I wonder if Vanessa would
take it from me. When I look
into her eyes, I find surprise.
Suspicion. Fear. Curiosity.

I wonder which of those
brought her to this place,
what monsters—internal or
external—she has fought.

I wonder what drives her
to give in to the goddess
of lust and sharp edges,
open her skin and bleed,

to purposely walk where most
digress, lost in the moment.
I wonder how it feels
to possess such courage.

⊥ Also Wonder

Why Vanessa got sick.
She looked fine just a few
seconds earlier. Of course,
she's not one to whine about

an upset stomach. Still,
the way her hands shook was
scary—kind of like how my
grandfather's used to betray him.

They say Parkinson's isn't
genetic, so it probably
won't ever affect my
athletic abilities,

or hinder my GPA.
But hey, knowing my luck,
I'll beat the odds and shimmy
my way into an early grave.

> *Mr. Sykes*, exhales Ms. Littell,
> *would you please share your words?*
> She sighs, and I try not to
> notice the view of her neckline.

I look down at what I've
written, smile. "I'm not sure
this is appropriate for
the rank and file. It's more

than a little suggestive."
I wait for her to read over
my shoulder, expect a
swift, negative reply.

Instead she says, *You are*
a skilled poet, gifted with
an ear for metaphor. This
is filled with passion. Read!

Guess I'll Excite Everyone

With my words. Oh, well, she
asked for it. I glance around
the room, face-to-face, find
unmasked inquisitiveness.

"My happiest memories
are sun-streaked afternoons
in the cinnamon arms of my
Emily—the evening star

glowing in a dusk-choked
sky. She wraps me in pleasure,
silent except for her
occasional sigh, and I

whisper, 'Keep me here,
beside you, where I can
breathe you in. Keep me
here, inside you, Emily.'

She makes no promises,
only tells me I can stay
for now. 'Sometimes it's good
to be lonely, good to feel

pain. But not now, my love.
Now I want you here beside
me, where you can breathe me in.
And I need you inside me.

You make me young again.'
Pressed against the curve
of her back, my fingers trace
the contours of one breast,

and then the other. Such
perfection in the texture
of her skin, sublime petals,
pressed into recollection.

My Emily."

Tony

Whoa, Baby!

Who the hell is Emily?
        If I were straight, I'd
have to get to know her.
        Think she has a brother?
Wonder why I haven't
        heard about her before.

The classroom breaks
        out in applause. "Damn,
Conner, could you make
        my poem look any
worse? Here I write about
        getting out of lockup

and you go and write
        about sex. Why didn't
I think about that?"
        Maybe I would have,
if sex for me had ever
        come close to that.

                        Conner's face flushes.
                                It was the best thing
                        that ever happened to me.

"So tell us more. Who
        is she? What does she
look like? Blond, I bet."

                        An odd smile creeps
                                across his face. *Yes,
                        she's blond. Everywhere.*

Things could get out
        of control, but Mr.
Hidalgo reins it in.

                *Okay, everyone. I
                        think we've heard
                enough about Emily.*

Now the room breaks
        out in a chorus of
boos. Mine is loudest.

Mr. Hidalgo Takes Control

Enough, already. Mr.
Ceccarelli, since
you seem to be so
communicative today,
I'm sure you've penned
a masterpiece. Please read.

I quit booing, clear
my throat. "I can't
write poetry, not like
Conner and Vanessa
can. All I have is some
words. Scrambled thoughts."

Ms. Littell comes over,
stands behind me, reads.
You have a lot more
here than scrambled
thoughts, and it's most
definitely poetry. Please share.

Here goes nothing.
          "Six years they took
away. Six years not
          allowed to say much
but 'Yes, sir; no, sir.'
          Today, I breathe a free

man's air, walk without
          sacrifice anywhere I
choose. A woman passes
          by. Without hesitation,
I say, 'Hello. Beautiful
          day, isn't it?' She turns

my way, smiles, a bright
          hint of hope that all
might one day be right
          in whatever world
tomorrow brings me."
          Still waiting for that.

No Applause

But I do get a couple
        Way to go's. Better
than total silence,
        anyway. And I guess
it was good to hustle
        up a halfway decent

memory. I had one
        or two others, but
they involved Phillip.
        These voyeurs might
like hearing about
        Conner's romantic

adventures, but I seriously
        doubt they'd want to hear
about Phillip and me.
        Anyway, that is a very
private part of my life,
        something I keep stashed

away and only withdraw
          in moments of weakness.
I'd rather share tales
          of Ma, the ol' dead ho',
or Larry the pervert,
          who got what he deserved.

                    Thank you for working
                              with me, says Ms. Littell.
                    I hope you'll all keep
                              writing. There's a lot
                    of talent in this room.
                              Please don't waste it.

Ms. Littell takes her leave,
          and it's on to algebra,
or in Conner's case,
          calculus. I think he knows
more about it than Mr.
          Hidalgo, but that's just my

uneducated opinion.

Vanessa

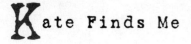ate Finds Me

In the bathroom.
The heaves are gone,
and I've blown my
insides out the other end.
My hands still shake
and I try to comfort
them with cool water.

*Dr. Starr heard you
weren't feeling well.*
Kate's tone is almost
apologetic. *She wanted
me to let you know it's
probably a side effect
of the lithium.*

I knew there were
side effects but didn't
realize they could be
so intense. Depression
is bad. This is worse.
My brain feels like it's
squishing through mud.
"Can I quit the lith?"

You have to give it
a chance. We'll reduce
the dosage until your
body adjusts. It might
take a few weeks.

Nausea. Diarrhea.
Tremors. Thick head.
Mouth like cotton balls.
"I need water. And I need
to lie down."

No Wonder

Mama refused to stay
on the lithium. Yes, she
was diagnosed bipolar,
with a tendency toward
schizophrenia. They tried
to correct her brain's mad
zigzag with medication.
But she was stubborn—swore
the only thing wrong
with her was her damnable
sidekick, the angel.

When they locked her up,
force-fed her pills,
she cleared up. Sooner
or later, they always let
her out, and she'd be
the mama we always
hoped she'd be.
For a few days.

That last day, she'd only
been out of the hospital
for a few hours.

Still had the bottle
of Xanax in her pocket.
The only problem
was she swallowed
a few too many.
One extra is one too
many. She yacked
down a half dozen.

Her doctors said
she wanted to die.
I thought so too.
And who was I
to argue?

My Own Overdose

Or whatever the problem is,
is making me sick again.
I don't want to go
to the bathroom, chance
prying eyes or questions.
So I lay very still
on my bed, give myself
to the thrashing
surf inside my body,
my brain.

Quick, Vanessa, think
of something still,
something serene.
Sand. I think of sand.
Lying on a thick carpet
of sand, somebody warm
beside me. My memory
holds Trevor. I replace
his face with Conner's.

Drowsy. I am drowsy
in his arms, feel his bloom
against the small of my back.

Like today. It is bright
in the desert sun—beneath
magic clouds of white.
Sucked into the white,
I give myself to Conner.
"Make love to me," I tell him.

And he answers,
*I can't deal with your
freaky mood swings,
Vanessa. One minute
you're solid, the next
you're like water.
Boiling water . . .*

It's Trevor's voice, and

I scream.

Conner

Thursday P.M.

Dr. Starr calls me to her
office, points me into a chair,
laces her fingers under
her chin. Where is this going?

> *Conner, I'm pleased with your*
> *progress,* the bulldog says.
> *But I really think we need*
> *to address the issue*
>
> *of your not wanting to go*
> *home for a visit this weekend.*
> *The Easter holiday provides*
> *connection with your family.*
>
> *I know that frightens you,*
> *but I don't know why. There's*
> *no history of abuse.*
> *Why shut yourself off from them?*

"You've got it all wrong. I'm
not afraid of going home.
It's just that I'm happier here,
where I don't have to evade

questions no one wants the
answers to. At least when *you*
ask me something, it's because
you want to know what I've

got to say. Mom and Dad
expect only what they want
to hear, and only then if
it's said with total respect.

Going home can only
lead to confrontation. Why
would I want that when I've
finally freed myself of it?"

As I Wait for Her Reply

I study her face, find an
odd blend of amusement
and understanding. But she
doesn't pretend sympathy.

> *You have to face them sometime,*
> *Conner. No parent is*
> *perfect, no child always right.*
> *Climb into their shoes, take*
>
> *an honest look at yourself.*
> *Do you like what you see?*
> *Can you try just a little to*
> *understand their point of view?*
>
> *Their son tried to kill himself—*
> *a parent's worst nightmare*
> *because they must accept blame.*
> *They want to forgive you, but first*
>
> *they have to forgive themselves.*
> *That's tough for anyone to do;*
> *for some, nearly impossible.*
> *Do you think they're strong enough?*

I just stare. How can she
be so dense? She's only met
them a time or two, but can't
she see through the pretense?

"You really don't get them at
all, Dr. Starr. Blame themselves?
Forgive themselves? For *my*
fall from grace? Not even!

My father can't be to blame.
He's never home long enough
to be an influence on me.
And Mom? If she ever took

responsibility for this,
what would her bridge club
think? Nope, the only person
they could blame at all is me."

We're Not Through Yet

Okay, Conner. And who do
you blame? Who do you think
is responsible for you?
She's made it a whole new game.

I've had plenty of time,
alone in my room, to
consider that very thing,
hours and hours to hone

my reply. "I blame Dad for
my drive for perfection.
He's always demanded
that Cara and I strive

to attain the highest grade,
highest score, to bring home
gold. A silver medal
meant losing, nothing more.

Mom I blame for making
me cold. What kind of
mother flat-out refuses
to hold her children, make

them feel wanted, warm, safe?
Emily made me feel all
those things and more. Is that
really so hard to understand?"

The bulldog's growl softens.
*No, of course it's not. But
surely you knew your affair
couldn't go on forever.*

"Forever has no meaning
when you're living in the
moment. I wasn't ready
for that moment to end."

Amen.

Tony

Easter Weekend

And the place has mostly
            cleared out. Aspen Springs,
graveyard. Kind of fitting,
            I guess. My dad asked
if I wanted to go visit
            him. Not ready for that.

Apparently, Conner wasn't
            ready to go home either.
He's sitting, staring
            at mindless television.
But I can tell he's not
            concentrating on the screen.

Unusual, considering
            this sitcom features
big-breasted women,
            with a minimum
amount of clothing
            covering their silicone.

"Hey, man. Damn quiet
            in here, huh?" I say.
"Kind of spooky."

Not as spooky as home,
              he answers. Besides,
I don't mind the quiet.

"Uh. Oh, sorry. Didn't
        mean to crowd your
space or anything."

No problem. Crowd
              my space. I'm done
brooding, anyway.

Brooding? Good word,
        one I've never once
used. "About what?"

Just thinking about
              home. Will I ever
want to go back there?

Carmella Bustles In

Hey, you two. Want
          some company? Looks
kind of lonely in here.
          She plops down on the
couch, very close to
          Conner, who doesn't move.

"You stuck here with
          us this weekend, Car?"
I measure her proximity
          to Conner, wonder if
she's flirting on purpose.
          "No place better to go?"

          She giggles. *What could*
                    be better than spending
          time with two gorgeous
                    guys? And, if you want,
          I've got permission to
                    take you out of here tomorrow.

Conner stirs, moves
        his leg even closer
to hers, just a fraction
        of an inch from brushing.
Out of here, where? Like
        maybe to San Francisco?

                Carmella laughs again.
                        I don't think we could
                get away with that.
                        But we can take in
                a movie. There are
                        some good ones playing.

"I'm in. But aren't they
        afraid we might overpower
you and hit the road?"
                        Don't even talk like
                                that. Someone might
                        take you seriously.

Someone Probably Should

But right now, I really
        have nowhere better
to go. And I wouldn't
        want to get Carmella
in trouble. Of course,
        I can't speak for Conner.

        But he seems cool
                with the plan. *Okay,*
   count me in too. A
            movie would be great.
   Unless you can figure
        a way to San Francisco.

           I'll work on that for
               next time. Meanwhile,
      can we please change
              the channel? Nothing
      worse than women
           with tits for brains.

Conner laughs. *Oh yeah,*
there are definitely worse
things than that. But I
wasn't watching this
show anyway. Here's
the remote. You choose.

It's really kind of scary,
        sitting here watching
TV with two people
        I like. Almost like
having a real family—
        not that I'd have a clue

what that was like.
        The closest I ever
came was Phillip.
        And he was so sick,
our time together
        so short, it almost

doesn't count.

Vanessa
Grandma's House

Feels completely
foreign, completely like home.
It's easier to breathe
here, where the walls
don't gather me in,
smother me in their arms.

> *Hey, Nessa, shouts Bryan,*
> *come in the kitchen.*
> *We're ready to color*
> *Easter eggs. If we mix*
> *blue and red, we'll get*
> *purple. Blue and yellow*
> *make green. Come here.*
> *I'll show you how.*

He's so excited to have
me back, he hasn't calmed
down for twenty seconds
since they picked me up,
yakking nonstop about
school and his new buddy,
Dean; about Cub Scouts
and popcorn fund-raisers.
"Be right there," I promise.

But first I need to take
a little detour. I've been
pocketing the lithium,
so I don't spend all three
days in the bathroom.
I'm not sick this afternoon,
but I feel a mad rush
of blue coming on.

And here I don't have
to use paper clips
or pop-tops. My trusty
razor blade is in its
cubby, calling
out to me. Just a little
slice, for old time's sake.

I Go into the Bedroom

Close the door,
remove my steel lover
from its place of honor
on the closet shelf.
I touch its stainless
tip to my index finger.
Sharp! Without pressure,
it draws a crimson bead.

Peel back my sleeve—
the one that covers
the barbed-wire scar,
affectionately place
the blade beneath
my left thumb. This
is the best rush
of all—the moment
right before the cut.
It's my decision now,
I'm in charge.
And just as I think
I'll give in to temptation,
reopen the old wound,

Bryan calls, *C'mon,*
Nessa, please? I'm
waiting for you.

I could still do it,
but I see my brother's
face, scream frozen
in place, and I put
the blade back
in its velvet sleeve.

"I'm coming right
now, Bryan. Save
some purple
dye for me."

The Kitchen

Is a Norman Rockwell painting—
Grandma, at the sink, draining
eggs; Bryan, at the table, drawing
wax pictures on cooled shells,
waiting for me to come help
with the dye. It's all so . . .
normal, something I rarely
feel. And I'm expected
to blend in, head
backstroking through blue.
I'm determined to do it too.

> *Look, Nessa. I put*
> *your name on this one.*
> *And I drew a train on it too.*

Bryan always did love
trains. Once Grandma took
us on the Amtrak, from Reno
to Sacramento. I was pretty
well bored out of my tree—
except for the cute guy
sitting across from me in
the observation car. And Bryan
loved it so much, how could
I possibly complain?

I saved lots of purple
for you. And all the other
colors too. I know! Let's
make a rainbow.

We go to work, dying
bands of blue, red,
and yellow. They bleed
a little, but so do rainbows.
Just as we're dipping the eggs
into the green,
the front door opens.
Grandma turns.
Bryan jumps up.
I can't believe my eyes.

"Daddy!"

Conner

Talk About Jumping

Through hoops! To get to go
to the movie, Tony and I
had to put in writing that
we know our privileges

will be suspended if we
so much as sneeze wrong.
And just to make sure, Dr.
Boston is coming along.

I suspect that's because she
has nowhere better to go—
no spring break for her, I guess.
Anyway, I'm happy to share

a bag of popcorn with
the delectable Dr. B.
I hope the movie's an R-
rated romp—something sexy

to fire up her pistons. "What
are we going to see?" I ask.
"A taste of Tarantino? Tim
Burton? Don't tell me Disney!"

Carmella laughs. *Heather
and I were thinking more
along the lines of Spielberg's
new sci-fi flick. Work for you?*

Dr. Boston is a Heather.
Sounds about right. And
as for Spielberg, well, we
just might catch sight of

someone curvaceous and
yummy, if not exactly
slutty. "Sure, works fine for
me. I'm easy to please."

We Take the Aspen Springs Limo

A minivan that must be
at least ten years old. It
wheezes along the icy road,
a decrepit old beast, and I

hope we make it the eight
miles to the theater.
Spring or no, it's much too
cold to walk it from here.

> Dahlia is with us too—
> another won't-go-home.
> *Da-hamn, it's cold out here,*
> *like a whole other planet.*

> *Weird,* says Tony, *how you*
> *disconnect from what's outside*
> *when you spend your life inside.*
> *I never know what to expect*
>
> *when I walk out the door. April,*
> *and snow on the ground. Do kids*
> *hunt Easter eggs in the snow? I*
> *was never a kid, so I don't know.*

"I only ever went to one
egg hunt," I answer. "Our
nanny took us because,
to be blunt, our parents

considered such frivolity
a total waste of time. Once
was more than enough for
me—that six-foot, pimply-faced

rabbit, leering like a lech,
wrecked me for weeks. Poor
Leona thought the experience
just might affect me for life."

Enough About Giant Bunnies

We reach the theater, all
in one piece, buy tickets, go
inside. Just as I think
this could turn into fun,

a familiar voice scratches
my eardrums. *Hey, Conner.*
What a surprise. I heard
you tried to die. That right?

"Hello, Kendra." Stiffly,
I turn around to face the
pretty blond cheerleader who
drowned in Emily's wake.

I consider the accident
excuse, but why even
go there? "Guess I did. Next
time I'll have to try harder."

Her face goes white. *Don't say*
that. Believe it or not, a few
people care about you. One
or two of us even love you.

Holy shit. How could she
love me? I dropped her like
a hot piece of tin. "I'm
sorry. I didn't mean it."

>   *There's Sean. Gotta go. Hope*
>   *to see you again soon, Conner.*
>   *Give me a call, if you want*
>   *to. I'm a good listener.*

I shuffle off to Screen
Three, settle beside Dr.
Boston, try to concentrate on
the black-humored movie, mind

on Kendra.

Tony
The Greatest Thing

About today is how
          normal I feel—like
totally mainstream. Okay,
          so I'm at the movies
with two crazy people,
          one lonely psychologist,

and one totally demented
          "house mother." At least
I'm *at* the movies, a place
          I've only been twice
before. And these freaky
          people feel like family.

                    Hey, Tony, says Dahlia,
                              check it out. That girl
                    has the hots for Conner.

The girl in question,
          a too-skinny blonde,
definitely knows
          Conner. He tells her
something and she
          looks ready to cry.

Jeez, man, what's up
          with that guy? Does
he have a magic wand?

"I suppose you could
          call it a wand," I answer,
and we both bust up.

          Carmella shimmies
                    up, arms loaded with
          buckets of popcorn and
                    oversize sodas. *Hurry*
          up! I hate missing
                    the start of a movie.

I Sit in Between

Carmella and Dahlia,
        passing popcorn and
laughing at how the girls
        hold their ears every
time the gunplay gets
        real loud. Too funny.

Every now and then
        I glance at Conner,
who's way too quiet
        to be enjoying himself.
Dr. Boston notices
        too. Even in the dark

of the theater, I see
        concern in the set of
her jaw. She leans over and
        whispers something, and
he shakes his head.
        Then it seems to me,

and I could be wrong,
            that she moves her knee
so it just touches Conner's.
            Now I don't know which
scene intrigues me more:
            the one on the screen,

or the one two seats away.
            I divide my attention
between the two and
            make a mental note
to ask Conner about
            the twig-thin blonde,

Dr. Boston, and Emily.
            Dahlia's right. His wand
must hold magic. For
            the first time in a long
time, I feel a tug in my
            own magic-free wand.

I Know I Should Wait

To ask Conner about
        any of that, but on
the way back to Aspen
        Springs, my mouth springs
open. "Hey, Conner.
        "Who was the cute blonde

at the movie theater?
        Someone you know?"
Everyone else stops
        babbling, waits for the
answer we all want to
        hear. It's slow coming.

                Finally, he says simply,
                    Kendra is an old girlfriend.
                We broke up a few months ago.

      Which should be good
              enough, but not for Dahlia.
      Why? What happened?

                I know Dr. B wants to
                    know. But she says, *That's*
          Conner's business, Dahlia.

I'm guessing, thinking
        back to his poem, it had
something to do with
        Emily. But Dr. Boston
is right. It's Conner's
        business, and he doesn't

seem inclined to share.
        Not that I won't ask
him again later. In
        private. When I try
to pry information
        about Dr. Boston and

Emily.

Vanessa

Bryan and I Rush

Into Daddy's arms—
tan and more muscled
than I remember. We kiss
him, all over his face,
from the apex of his buzz cut
to the scrub on his chin.
Finally, he pushes us away.

> *Okay, okay. I'm happy*
> *to see you, too. And I've*
> *missed my crew. Stand*
> *back and let me get*
> *a good look at you.*

His eyes measure us,
head to toe, as Grandma
goes to him, gently
touches his shoulder.
Good to have you home,
Ron. Good to have you,
all in one piece.

> Daddy stands, pulls
> Grandma to him.

No need to worry about that, Mama. No need at all. I still got all my limbs, and all my wits. But, my God, how these children have grown, and grown up.

Grown up? Me? I suppose I have. Killing things, and almost killing myself, must have changed me some, after all.

I'm Glad

I put away my blade,
untested. Daddy would have
noticed, of that I'm sure.
He and blood are buddies.
Grandma's right. It's good
to see him, all in one piece.
When your father's always
knee-deep in a conflict
somewhere, you can never
be certain if—or how—
you'll see him again.

> *C'mon, Daddy, we're*
> *coloring Easter eggs.*
> *There's no Easter Bunny,*
> *you know, so we've got*
> *to hide them ourselves.*
> Bryan gave up on the Easter
> Bunny last year. This year
> he'll probably give up
> on Santa, too. Lost faith.
> Makes me sad.

Be right there, son,
soon as I put my things
in my room. Dad pauses,
looks me square in the eye.
You and I need to talk. Later.

Apprehension grips my
throat. "S-sure."
I watch my daddy stride
down the hall, one burly
arm swinging his heavy
knapsack, and, despite
a healthy dose of fear
about what he has to say
to me, I inflate with pride.

Later

After a scrumptious
Grandma-style three-course
dinner, Daddy sends Bryan
and me to our rooms.

> *So I can think about*
> *stashing Easter eggs,*
> he tells Bryan.

But I know he wants to
talk to Grandma in private.
I leave my door cracked,
hoping to hear snatches
of their conversation. I do.

> *Why didn't you tell me*
> *about this . . . cutting thing?*
> asks Daddy.

> *What could you have*
> *done, Ron? I didn't know*
> *myself, until it was almost . . .*
> Grandma's voice cracks.

And I left you to deal with
Margaret, too. I'm sorry, Mama,
I didn't think . . . didn't realize . . .
I mean, I knew she was sick.
But I had no idea she would
do such a terrible thing.

None of us guessed she
was so far over the edge.
I'm just glad I was the one
who found her.

Have the kids gone to visit her?

I can almost hear
Grandma shake her head.

We all will, then.

Tomorrow.

Conner

Dinner Tonight

Was McDonald's, on the way
back from the movie. Quarter
Pounders and fries—way to
pack on empty calories.

Now Tony, Dahlia, Carmella,
and I are sitting around,
cutting major farts. Dahlia
doesn't even try to stifle hers.

Ugh! says Tony. *Girl, you'll
never catch a man like that.
And by the way, didn't your ma
ever tell you to say, "'Scuse me"?*

*You oughta know 'bout catching
men, freak. And I did say excuse
me, with my butt. Apparently
you don't speak "rectum."*

Everyone cracks up, except
me. Nothing is funny
tonight. My mood wants to
swing between reflective

and halfway terrified.
I'm afraid—a strange thing
to say, but true—that despite
whatever progress I've made,

when I get out of this place,
everything will be exactly
the same as before—even me.
I'll still live in my parents'

shadow; I'll still drive myself to
achieve impossible perfection.
And I'll never let myself
believe someone really loves me.

Two Ativans Toward Sleep

I lie in bed, listen to
the grind of wind against
cinder-block walls. I'm not
sure how to unwind this coil

of images flashing inside
my brain. Some are "borrowed"
from the flick we saw today:
good people, slain by evil

automatons; the slightly
effeminate hero (and why
does *he* come to mind?);
the geeky alien zero—

apparently, advanced
civilizations send them
off in their latest spacecraft
to defend home and planet.

The meds kick in and here
comes the princess—all curves,
in a tight blue dress. Blue . . . tight . . .
Heather. Pretty name. Sums

her up completely. Oops . . .
transformation, titian hair
bleaching blond, gray eyes tinting
blue—Kendra, sweet temptation.

Some of us love you, she whispers,
tossing her long, golden hair.
Why can't you love back, Conner?
What the hell's wrong with you?

I want to blame Mom, Dad,
Emily, and I do. But
there's someone else, too,
in a sliver of memory.

Easter Sunday Morning

I wake, not exactly refreshed.
Despite the meds, I tossed
and tumbled, caught in the claws
of a dream-disturbed night.

Beyond the window glass,
a silver glint stabs my eyes.
I turn on my side, refuse
to budge, no hint of sound

outside my room. All this
silence, wrapped around Sunday
morning, reminds me of home.
Now I feel trapped beneath

my blankets. I throw them off,
stomp to the door, stick my head
out in the hall. "I have to pee."
Nothing. I don't know what's in store

for me if I go without
permission. But I really have
no choice. I pad to the bathroom,
hope my morning "condition"

will allow me to pee after all.
I'm still waiting for "deflation"
when Tony walks through the door.
He gives me a prime once-over.

Hey man. Nice firewood. He grins,
then looks away and changes
the subject. *Kind of creepy
today, with nobody here.*

Totally shriveled, I finish
my business. "Must be somebody
here, somewhere." I wash
my hands, splash the crust from

my eyes.

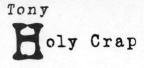

Tony
Holy Crap

It's the first time I've
          seen Conner exposed,
and boy, what exposure!
          The guy is built like
a mule. No wonder
          women lust after him.

I'm lusting a little,
          myself, but manage to
keep it in check, except
          one comment about
his wood. A guy likes
          to know he's appreciated.

I watch him splash
          his face. Cold water, I bet,
proving himself macho.

                              Damn, that's cold! He
                                        catches my smile in the
                              mirror. *What's so funny?*

"Nothing. Just thinking
          about yesterday. Carmella
was funnier than shit."

Conner drops his defensive
                    stance. *Yeah, she was. Too bad
I wasn't in the mood to laugh.

He opens the door.
        "We noticed. What was
up with you, anyway?"

                    Up comes the wall again.
                            *I don't know. Maybe they
need to up my meds again.*

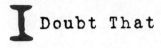 Doubt That

But know better than
        to say so. "Well, I'm
catching a shower.
        Carmella said we can
go to church in Reno
        this morning. Going?"

> *I don't know. Maybe.*
> *   Guess it's better than*
> *sticking around here,*
> *   playing with . . . uh . . .*
Something close to
        panic fills his eyes.

"Your firewood?" I laugh
        and Conner has to, too,
or look like a total fool.

> *I'd better get dressed.*
> *   See you at breakfast. It*
> *smells pretty good today.*

I turn the faucet to
            steamy, step under,
and let its hot fingers
            touch me all over,
trying not to think
            about the last time

hot fingers (real ones)
            touched me all over.
It's Easter, the holiest
            of holy days, and at
the moment I'm feeling
            like a world-class sinner.

My brain tells me it's
            all wrong, the way
my body's responding
            to thinking about sex,
the last time I had it, and
            when I might have it again.

Not Quite Free

But out from behind
        locked doors, for
the second day in a
        row, it doesn't
even matter that it's
        snowing—on Easter.

> Dahlia's pissed. *We get*
>   *enough of this Jesus junk*
> *every other Sunday.*

But Paul had to drive
        'cause Carmella freaks
when it snows. So it
        was all of us, or none
of us. And Conner and I
        voted, two to one, to go.

> Carmella chose the church.
>   *I don't do Catholic anymore,*
> *not since I got divorced.*

Twenty-three and divorced
        already! At least she doesn't
have kids. (I don't think.)
        We turn into a crowded
parking lot, and I notice
        Conner begin to squirm.

                    Here? he says. *Do we*
                            have to go to this one?
                    His eyes scan the cars,
                            settle on a black Lexus.
                    They're here, he says.
                            I can't go in. No way.

"Who's here?" I ask,
        but I suspect the answer,
and it's quick to come.

                    My family.

Vanessa
All Dressed Up

In the best of our best
Sunday clothes, Bryan,
Grandma, and I pile
into the rented SUV, wait
for Daddy. Finally, he comes
out the door, in full-dress
uniform, boots spit-polished
until they shine like satin.
He doesn't wear a smile.

> *I'd forgotten it snows*
> *here in April. I thought*
> *I'd left that behind,*
> *in that godforsaken*
> *place. Hell, I bet even*
> *Allah doesn't go there.*
> *Oh, well, we'll make the best*
> *of it, I guess. Ready?*

No! I'm not ready. I want
to go back to Aspen Springs,
where it's safe, predictable.
Where my secrets and I
can hang out, undisturbed.

I don't want to go see her,
not there. No one belongs
there, just like no one
belongs in Afghanistan,
if Daddy's word can be
trusted. And I have to
trust it. Don't I?

*All right, then. Here we
go. The O'Reilly family,
all together again.*

Almost all together,
he means.

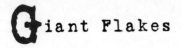iant Flakes

Of heavy, wet snow splat
against the windows.
Daddy cruises slowly,
and I understand he doesn't
want to go where
we're going either.
It's a duty thing.

Thank God for the lithium.
It really seems to have
kicked into gear the last
couple of days. My hands
still shake sometimes,
and my mouth is dry
most of the time,
but it is easier to hover
up out of the blue.

> Dad took me aside earlier,
> while Grandma helped
> Bryan get dressed.

Nessa, girl, I know it's
been tough, trying to take
your mother's place,
'specially seeing her at
her worst and all. I want
you to know that she was
a real good woman, when
she wasn't in a bad space.

"I know, Daddy."

You'll be a fine woman
too. We'll get you the help
you need, hear me? I don't
want to lose you, too.

I'd never seen him so soft
before. It wasn't what
I'd expected, and it grabbed
my breath away.
He pulled me into him,
where I couldn't see him cry.
But I could feel him tremble.

He's Hard Again Now

And I wonder how soft
he'd be if I confessed
how I left Mama, blank
eyed, in a pool of overdose-
induced peace.
My arm twitches and, lithium
or no, I want to open a vein,
bleed out the guilt.

> *Your grandmother tells me*
> *you'll go into a wilderness*
> *survival program soon,*
> says Daddy.

> *Really?* says Bryan. *Cool!*

"I guess so," I answer, not
sure what "soon" means.
"That's Level Four, the last
step before I come home."

> *You've never done anything*
> *like that, have you?*

The closest I've come is
a hike in the woods with
Grandma and Bryan. "No."

When the time comes, you
cowboy up. You're tough,
just like your father.

"No one's as tough as you,
Daddy. But I'll try."

Oh. Here we are.

He slows to a crawl and we
turn into a snow-covered parking
lot. Everything around us is gray
stone, frosted white. Spooky. My
heart falls into my tummy. Tough?

Not me.

Conner

Almost May

The weather warms, the hills
start to thaw, and I can run
the perimeter of the big
fenced compound. My heart pumps

against the scar on my chest,
bare beneath the afternoon sun.
Tony catches up, and I push
harder, dare him to keep up.

Surprise. He can. Not only
that, but he's a lot more buff
than I would have expected, and
completely at ease with my pace.

> *Mind if I run with you? It's*
> *good to be challenged. I used*
> *to run every day in lockup.*
> *I should have kept at it.*

"You're still in decent shape.
Did you lift in lockup too?"

> *Yeah, and at the gym when I got*
> *out. For a few months, anyway.*

At the gym? I had the idea
Tony was a basic street kid.

> *But after Phillip died, it was*
> *all I could do just to eat.*

"Phillip? Who was Phillip?"
Boyfriend? Brother? Uncle?

> *He was half foster father,*
> *half my best friend in the world.*

We run in silence for another
three laps. Hard. Harder. Side
by side in friendly rivalry,
till we're ready to collapse.

We Hit the Shower

To wash off some well-deserved
sweat. Tony makes a point of
looking the other way, but I
haven't felt uncomfortable yet,

being naked around him.
Stanley is much creepier.
That boy should not be allowed
to touch himself with soapy hands.

"So, Tony. How was your visit
to your dad's?" Dr. Boston
talked him into it—it's a
prerequisite for wilderness camp,

one I have to face myself,
before long. After my gutless
performance on Easter, I wonder
if I can score the balls.

> *It went okay, I guess. He's got
> a sweet house at Tahoe—not huge,
> but more than I'm used to, on a
> street with its own private beach.*

His wife, Talia, is nice, not real
bright, but what could you expect
from someone who fell in love
with my dad? She was polite,

and a real good cook. No wonder
Pa married her! 'Course, if she
doesn't quit cooking pasta, he'll
end up buried before his time.

"Pasta, till death do us part.
A slice of Italian-American
life." We laugh, but I think
that price isn't so dear for

a few good years together,
well fed and otherwise
satisfied. Nothing at all
to dread about that scenario.

It's Better Than What I've Got

To face at home. Two cold people,
who can't remember why they
fell in love in the first place. If
they were ever in love. I chew

on that as we dry off, get dressed.
"Did your dad ever really love
your mom?" I ask. But I'm
betting he'll go to bat for love.

> *Well, yeah. At least I think so.*
> *Hell, maybe not. Fuck, Conner.*
> *Maybe there's no such thing. Lots*
> *of people rot, waiting for it.*

Okay, I was wrong. It's weird,
how Tony and I are on
the same page, with some
regularity. "You don't

by some remote chance happen
to be a Republican?"

> *Uh. No. I'm not into politics.*
> *Why? Are you—a Republican?*

I stop and think—really think.
"My parents are steadfast
conservatives. So maybe I'm
a Dem after all." (Probably not.)

> Good to know. Because any
> "party" that shuts its doors
> on the poor, gay, or otherwise
> "useless" gets my hearty F.U.

Right on. If I ever actually
grow big enough *huevos* to chance
a visit home, I'll consider
letting them know I've become

a Democrat.

Tony

I Don't Tell Conner Everything

About last weekend.
        Like how, despite all
Pa did to make me feel
        at home, I was a complete
stranger under his roof,
        and I doubt that will change.

How the big bed in
        the spotless wine red
bedroom made me feel
        lonelier than ever. I've
never, not even once
        in my life, slept in a bed

like that—so much room,
        such heavy, warm covers,
deep, fluffy pillows. I felt
        like I was drowning in
comfort, choking on the idea
        I could ever belong there.

How even though I
        had plenty of meds,
supplied by Aspen
        Springs, I sneaked into
Talia's bathroom,
        borrowed a Valium or three.

Pop a Valium with a
        Prozac, you don't care
where you are, or who's
        talking in the other
room, not even if you
        know they're talking

about you. At least
        the combination put
me in a place where
        it was easy to keep
my big mouth shut.
        Who needs confrontation?

Apparently, Stanley Does

He's in a mood at group
        this afternoon, and it's
going to be hella
        interesting because
the person he's set on
        taking on is Dr. Starr.

> *Life is all about choices,*
>   the bulldog says. *Let's*
> *talk about the choices*
>   *you'll make when you*
> *leave Aspen Springs. Where*
>   *will you go from here?*

> Stanley leans his chair
>   back on two legs, sticks
> a finger up his nose. *I'm*
>   *gonna go find me a cute*
> *little girl and show her*
>   *the business end of Stanley.*

First, I suggest you sit
             that chair back down
on four legs. Now tell
             us what you meant.
Usually, "the business
             end" refers to a weapon.

Stanley stands, smiling
                as his right hand falls
        toward his zipper.
                That's right. And
        this right here is my
                weapon of choice.

Damn if he doesn't
        yank his ugly little
thing right out of his
        pants. The girls scream,
Dr. Starr's eyes go huge,
        and Stanley starts to laugh.

No One Dares Come Between

Stanley and his target,
        except for Vanessa,
sitting smack in his path.

> *Come on, Stanley*, she says.
>   *You don't really want to*
> *mess with Dr. Starr, do you?*

Is she crazy? That fat
        fuck will go right
over the top of her.

> *Stay out of this, bitch,*
>   *or I'll take you out*
> *too*, promises Stanley.

> Everyone pushes back
>   into the wall as I start
> toward Vanessa. But before
>   I can get close, Conner
> plants himself right in front
>   of Stanley. *Far enough.*

Stanley stops, but only
            for a second. He raises
his hands, fists tight.
            I'm not afraid of you,
preppie. Get the hell
            out of my way.

Dr. Starr moves toward
      the door, knowing help
lies not far beyond.
            But Conner takes control,
                  warning, *Just give me an*
            excuse to kick your ass.

Believe it or not, Stanley
      does, moving straight
into Conner, swinging.
      Conner lifts a defensive
arm, knocks Stanley off
      balance, takes a swing of

his own.

Vanessa

OMG!

Conner is so incredible.
In one movement, he drops
Stanley to the floor
like a swatted fly.
Paul and Stephanie rush
through the door,
but the whole ugly
confrontation is over.
They drag Stanley,
sobbing and slobbering,
to his feet, shriveled
penis still exposed.

> *Put him in isolation,*
> says Dr. Starr. *I'll call*
> *juvenile detention.*
> *The rest of you can go*
> *back to your rooms.*
> *We're finished for today.*
> *Conner, may I speak*
> *with you for a minute?*

I hold back while
the others start toward
the door. I want to take
in Conner, barely breathing
hard after playing hero.
I watch Dr. Starr's fingertips
rest lightly on his shoulder,
and I fight a jealous shiver.

          He's fine, isn't he?

"Tony! You scared
the bejesus out of me!"

          Sorry. But he is fine,
          isn't he?

"Yes, he is." Suddenly,
I notice I'm floating
in a cloud of white.

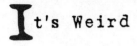t's Weird

Because since I've been
on the lithium, I haven't
gone manic at all, although
I have fallen back into the blue
zone several times.
Dr. Starr says
lithium works faster
against the white.

Yet here I am, feeling
fearless (which explains
my earlier lunacy—Stanley
could have knocked me
senseless); feeling stimulated
(by the hysteria and close
call, but more by Conner,
standing up for me, standing
close to me); feeling alive
(straddling the razor wire).

> *You're blushing,*
> whispers Tony.
> *What have you got*
> *on your mind, Vanessa?*

"Like you can't guess."
Oh yes, it's on my mind—
Conner, lying with me
in a bed of tall, cool
grass. Conner, leaning
over me, his long,
lean body exposed.
Conner, kissing me
with his luscious mouth . . .

> *Here he comes. You*
> *might want to close*
> *your mouth.*
> *You're drooling.*

A Slight Exaggeration

At least I think so.
I circle my lips with
my tongue, hoping
to catch any stray drool,
as Conner comes very close.

> He reaches out, touches
> my cheek. *You okay?*

My heart threatens
implosion, but I manage
to fake cool. "Just fine.
Thank you, Conner."

> He shrugs. *No problem.*
> *He had it coming.*

> *What did the bulldog*
> *want?* asks Tony. *You*
> *in any trouble?*

> *Nah. She thought*
> *he had it coming too.*
> *Hey, who knew Stanley*
> *had the balls?*

*Balls? You mean you
could see them, too?*

We all crack up and Dr. Starr
clears her throat. "I think that's
a hint. We'd better go."
Tony leads the way.

Conner falls in, very close behind me.
You have to be more careful,
he whispers. *I won't always
be around to protect you.*

His voice is chocolate—
sweet, smooth, rich . . .

. . . foreboding.

Conner

Actually, Dr. Starr

Wanted to strongly suggest
I go home this weekend.

*You're ready, Conner. You
are stronger than you know.*

"Why do you say that? Because I
took care of Stanley? He's nothing
but mouth. But home? I'm afraid
of there. Too many judgments."

*You want to get out of here
sometime, don't you? Our next
Challenge program starts in two
weeks. Chew on that for a while.*

So I'm chewing. I do want
to get out, but where, oh where,
will I go from here? I've always
looked forward to senior year,

varsity football, cheerleaders'
panties. But I can't go back
to school now. Everyone thinks
I'm some kind of nut, and fuck,

they're right. I am. I've been
here, trying to get a handle
on my craziness, for months.
But, despite all their prying,

Drs. Starr and Boston are
not even close to fixing me.
If I told them every secret,
an overdose of stinking truth,

would they break down and
admit I'm damn near as warped
as Stanley? That's an eye-
opener and, shit, it's true.

But Hey, Guess What

Crazy means I'm not liable
for my actions. So screw it,
I'll go home, propped up on
Prozac against distractions

like my mom and dad bitching
at me, Cara, and each other;
like Mom and Dad quizzing me
about school, my future and Emily,

certainly not in that order.
Meanwhile, I'm going to catch
up with Vanessa. Someday
I want more than her smile.

Does that mean there's hope
for me after all? She doesn't
have a single crow's-foot, no
cigarette taint to her laughter.

A wedge of crazies shuffles
along the corridor, and
Vanessa and Tony walk
slowly, at the rear of the throng.

I watch Vanessa sway her hips
and a sudden urge comes over
me. Not liable for my
actions, I surge straight ahead,

push my body against hers.
She slows even more, letting
me nest against her, as if she
knows what I've got in mind.

I lift her hair, bend, and drop
my lips to her neck, kiss
the soft pulse behind her ear.
She slips her hand into mine.

   Mmm. She sighs, and I know
   she wants to kiss me back.
But this is not the place. "Soon,"
I promise her. Very soon.

Tony Tosses a Jealous Look

Over his shoulder. Weird, but
I get the feeling he isn't
jealous of Vanessa. Somehow,
he seems jealous of me.

"Hey, Tony," I test. "I'll give you
a kiss too, if you say please."

> *You wish*, he jabs. *But I prefer
> a man who likes to be on top.*

"Ouch, little brother! I like
it on top. And on the bottom.
And standing up. And . . . Oh, man,
I gotta stop or go jerk off!"

> *Oh, yech*, says Vanessa, but
> she says it with a laugh. *Guys
> are just the nastiest creatures.
> Don't the two of you agree?*

> Tony slips right into "gay."
> *Of course, you luscious girl.
> And that's how I love 'em—
> nasty, sweaty, meaty and coarse.*

"That's how I like my women,
too." Too brave. Vanessa's
scowl could cut me in half.
I backpedal, fast. "Except you!"

We reach the gender T—
boys go right, girls straight ahead,
past the rec room. Vanessa
stops to blow two kisses—one

toward Tony, the other to me,
and I think maybe I could learn
to love someone, after all.
I drink the thought, try hard

to swallow it.

Tony

Three Days

Since they hauled Stanley
            away and now, I hear,
he'll be back this afternoon.
            His parents must have way
deep pockets. That dude
            should be locked up like

Hannibal Lecter—behind
            shatterproof glass, so
science might have a
            chance to discover some
unidentified mental defect.
            Stanphrenia. Yeah, that's it.

Oh well, he'll be Level
            One again, so I may not
have to see him, long
            as I go to the Challenge.
Some people here are
            afraid to go. Not me.

A few weeks climbing
            obstacles, sleeping outside,
building fires without
            matches, and eating out
of cans? Sounds about
            like living on the street.

Six of us are eligible
            for the Challenge now—
Lori, Dahlia, Justin,
            Vanessa, Conner, and me.
Well, Conner will be,
            if he makes it through

this weekend. I don't
            know exactly what's
waiting for him at home.
            I just know he's a lot
more scared of there than
            he is of obstacle courses.

I Wish I Could Be a Mirror

On one of those walls, but
        I can't, so I'll head on
over, see if I can talk
        to Vanessa, who's reading
in the rec room. The other
        girls are yakking nearby.

They never ask Vanessa
        to sit with them. Or if they
do, she always says no
        thanks. She's a worse
loner than I am. Not as
        bad as Conner, though.

Loner or no, I plop
        down beside her. "Hey,
you. Whatcha reading?"
        Even before she looks up,
I can see her smile, in
        the corners of her eyes.

Finally she lifts her
          gaze from her book,
and her smile is worth
          a thousand words.
Hey, Tony. Thanks
          for saying hi. It was

feeling lonely in this
          noisy room. You always
seem to know when I
          could use a friend. Sit
down, okay? Her warm
          hand finds mine, pulls.

I sit very close to her,
          and I'm glad when she
doesn't take away her hand.
          It's warm. Soft. Girly.
Like in the movies,
          I lift it, kiss softly.

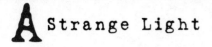 Strange Light

Fills Vanessa's eyes.
        Confusion? Clarity?
Disgust? "What? You
        never had a guy kiss
you before? Oh, yeah. You
        did. I saw, remember?"

            She smiles. *I'm not
                    quite senile yet,
            dear. To answer your
                    question, yes, I've had
            lots of guys kiss me. Just
                    none quite like you.*

"Quite like me, meaning
        gay?" I pretend hurt.
"And what do you mean,
        'lots of guys'? Can you
quantify that for me?"
        My turn to smile.

"Lots of guys," meaning
            too many—I didn't
even like all of them.
            Now she brings my
hand to her kiss. "Quite
            like you," meaning special.

Tony, no one in here,
            including Conner, treats
me with the kind of respect
            and friendship that you
do. Anyway, all "gay"
            means to me is happy.

"It doesn't mean that
            to me, Vanessa. My
lifestyle has caused
            a lot of pain. I hope
to change that when
            I get out of here."

I do?

Vanessa

Tony Is So Different

From what I thought
him to be, the first few times
I was around him.
Initial impression: funny,
not particularly intelligent,
homosexual to the point
of caricature.

Current impression:
funny, way smart, and not
just street smart;
sensitive but strong. Gay?
Maybe, but there is a definite
attraction between us.
And gay, straight, or somewhere
in-between, I love him.

Suddenly, I want to tell him.
"I love you, Tony."
I expect a smart-ass reply,
or at least surprise. But
I'm the one who's surprised.

I love you, too, Vanessa,
and in my life, love is rare.
You are rare—someone who
bothered to scratch under
my skin and find the person
beneath. No one else ever
did that, except for Phillip.
But I don't have him to
fall back on anymore.

"Tell me about Phillip,"
I say, "and I want to know
everything. How did you meet?
Were you a couple?
Did you love him, too?"

He spends the next half hour
telling me all about Phillip.
I'm glad he was Tony's friend.
I wish I had a friend like that.
Or maybe I do.

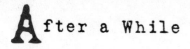
After a While

The conversation veers
toward Conner. Why is he
always on both of our minds?
"You and Conner seem
pretty tight lately," I say.
"I think I'm jealous."

>   *Of me or him?* Tony jokes.
>   *Either way, no worries.*
>   *We haven't made out yet.*
>   *I have seen him in the shower,*
>   *though. Mm, mm, mm.*

"Now I *know* I'm jealous."
We laugh, but the picture
of Conner in the shower,
water streaming down
over his muscular body,
lodges in my brain.

>   *You like him a lot, huh?*
>   *I do too, but not in the way*
>   *you think. And I'm not*
>   *really sure why. He's*
>   *not easy to get close to,*
>   *not easy to understand.*

"It's not easy to get
close to anyone in here,
Tony. Everyone's afraid
of everybody else . . . maybe
because we're all afraid
of ourselves."

Tony mulls that over, nods.
You know, I think
you've got a great future
ahead of you—as a psychologist.
But I'm not afraid of one
person—you. I hope we can
stay friends when we get
out of here.

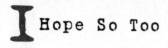

I Hope So Too

And I tell him so, but then
admit, "My grandma will
be good with it, but my dad
probably won't understand.
He thinks gay people are freaks."

> *But you don't think*
> *that way. Why not?*

I shrug. "I take people
at face value. Besides, you
don't have to be gay to be
a freak. Just look at me."

> *Being bipolar doesn't*
> *make you a freak.*

"Sometimes it does, Tony.
Sometimes it does."

> *I think you're just*
> *about perfect, Vanessa.*

I glance down, notice
we've been holding
hands this entire time.
"I've been pretty screwed
up for a while. But I feel
a little less freaky, now the lithium
is starting to work, and the side
effects aren't as bad."

> *I'm feeling better too.*
> *Like maybe there's a place*
> *for me—a place I might even*
> *want to be. Phillip told me*
> *there was, but after he died,*
> *I didn't want to look for it.*

"I understand." And I do.
Death can do that

to you.

Conner

Home Sweet Home

I've never really thought
about how it looked before—
it was just the place I ate
and slept. But now, sitting

in Mom's Lexus, parked in
the wide, curved driveway, I
stare at the oversized Tudor,
decide it's truly obnoxious.

Maybe it's because I've lived
in a tidy, cell-like room
for the past dozen weeks, but
"home" looks more like a hotel

than a house—sprawling, coiffed
and manicured, impersonal
as hell. Four people, living
in five thousand square feet? Absurd!

Mom chauffeured, assaulting
me with regulations: *No phone
calls; no unsupervised jaunts;
no meds. My expectations*

are high that you can return
to a normal life. That won't
happen if you're constantly
stoned. Are you strong enough

to make it through a weekend
without propping yourself up
on antidepressants? Her eyes
reflected a boatload of doubt.

I shrugged, kept my mouth shut.
Nothing I could have said—at
least, nothing totally true—
would have made her feel better.

She's Standing

Just inside the front door,
waving for me to come on.
I guess I'd better, before she
turns into a raving bitch.

The lawn is greening, and in
the flower beds, bevies
of tulips and daffodils nod
colorful heads. It's all so

cheerful I want to heave. On
the step, I turn, hoping to
catch a glimpse of someone
familiar, jogging by. Nothing.

I stare hard down the block,
don't find her car in her driveway.

> *Would you please come inside?* hisses
> Mom. *Are you out of your mind?*
>
> *That woman doesn't live there
> anymore. Did you think she would?*

Anger flares. "Why wouldn't she,
Mother? What the hell did you do?"

*What did I do? The real blame
lies with you. Your father and I
simply suggested to her it
might be wise to move elsewhere.*

"Emily wouldn't cave in and go
because of a simple suggestion.
Threat is more like it, huh, Mom?
Must you always use your claws?"

*Call it what you will, Conner.
With that temptation gone,
it's safe for you to come home.
End of explanation.*

Of course. It's her favorite
expression. I feel the serious
need for Prozac before
depression overwhelms me.

Not Exactly a Warm, Fuzzy Welcome

Although I didn't really
expect hugs, kisses, and a
surprise welcome home
party. Still, such direct

affirmation of my parent's
power wielding is scary.
Two "beautiful people" who
devour opponents like bread.

Mom disappears and I start
down the long hall, lined with
photos and trophies. Suddenly
I'm a small child, looking up at

my parents' accomplishments,
knowing I'm expected to hang
my own on the wall, knowing
I can never climb high enough.

Upstairs, I hear Cara's music.
Won't she come say hello?
I veer left, into the sunken
living room, expecting to see

white Berber carpet, perhaps
with a hint of a rust-colored
stain. The carpet is a pale
shade of mint—totally new.

Pretty, isn't it? Mom, come
to check up on me. *I decided
I didn't want white, after all. Will
you please put away your things?*

I pick up the overnight bag,
start toward the kitchen. Part of me
wants to confront Mom. The bigger
part just wants water, to push

the Prozac down.

Tony

Orientation for the Challenge

Begins today. Mr. Hidalgo
        says we have to finish up
for-credit work before we
        can "go climb rocks and
swing from ropes." Sounds
        like Boy Scouts to me.

                    It's not exactly Boy Scouts,
                            says Sean, a Challenge
                    counselor. *More like Swiss*
                            Family Robinson, in the
                    high desert. You'll have
                            limited water (just enough

                    to drink—you'll stink
                            before you're through,
                    believe me.) Food is MREs—
                            Meals, Ready to Eat, military
                    style. Think chicken, potato,
                            and vegetable mush. Mmm!

Vanessa shoots a "gag me"
         finger and a huge smile.
Can't wait! she mouths,
         glancing at Conner, who
sits off by himself. He's
         been lost in himself since

his visit home last weekend.
         Vanessa and I have both
grilled him about it, but
         all he'll say is, *Nothing
has changed. It's exactly
         the same and always will be.*

At least my dad's home is
         something all new. I might
even stay awhile, until
         one of us decides we've
made a major mistake—
         or my birth certificate has.

Meanwhile, Sean and Raven

Tell us all about how to
        prepare for the Challenge.
They say to toughen up
        mentally; that if we do,
the physical part will
        take care of itself. Uh-huh.

        Wilderness survival is mind
                over matter, says Raven,
      who's probably the strongest
            woman I've ever seen.
        Thirst. Hunger. Fatigue.
                All originate in the brain.

More accurately, the body's
        reaction to them originates
in the brain. But I'll just
        keep quiet. They've already
warned us about thinking
        we know more than they do.

We won't put you in harm's
           way, adds Sean, *although*
it may seem like it from time
           to time. And we do expect
you to push yourselves
           almost to the point of pain.

No pain, no gain—an old,
           very warped philosophy.
But after weeks and weeks
           of listening to people
gripe about their phobias,
           complexes, and manic episodes,

not to mention abuse, neglect,
           and molestation by relatives,
priests, neighbors, and stepparents,
           one-on-one with
the wilderness sounds like
           a vacation to sanity.

Sean and Raven Leave

Manuals and study guides,
       to read in our spare time.
"Hey, Conner," I try, hoping
       to pull him into the moment.
"Ever seen a rattlesnake,
       up close and personal?"

               He looks up from his lap.
                  Only my mother, the nasty,
             sidewinding bitch. You?

"Yeah, I saw one once.
       Poor, stupid snake crawled
out on the freeway. Ugly!"

            We won't see any snakes,
                 guesses Vanessa. Or, if we
            do, they'll be moving slow.

"How do you know? Are
       you some kind of a herp . . .
herpe . . . snake expert?"

Not an expert, but I did
have an interest in school.
Maybe I'll take up herpetology
if I ever make it to college.
All I know is it's still pretty
cold at night for reptiles.

"It's still pretty cold at night
        for people, too, at least if
you have to sleep outside.
        I slept outside in a blizzard
once. Wouldn't go
        looking to do that again."

                I did that once, too, admits
                        Vanessa, *because my boyfriend*
                wanted to. Stupid, huh?
"The things we do for love . . .
        well, sweetie, I'd sleep
outside *naked* in a blizzard,

for you."

Vanessa

We're Up to Our Elbows

In schoolwork, Challenge study,
red tape, counseling sessions,
and visits from home—all
to make sure we're prepared
for the "experience of our lives,"
not to mention what will follow:
going home, back to our families,
friends, schools, and hangouts.
The very things that put us here
to begin with. Am I ready?

> Dr. Starr wants to know.
> *Are you ready to leave*
> *Aspen Springs, Vanessa?*
> *Even beyond that, you'll be*
> *eighteen in a few months.*
> *Can you take responsibility*
> *for yourself, live on your own,*
> *and deal with your BPD?*

"I don't know," I admit.
"But I've got to take care
of myself sooner or later.
I know the lithium is working,
at least most of the time.

I hardly ever swing manic
anymore. Sometimes I do
feel depressed, but not near
as much as I used to."

> *What about your mother?*
> *Are you ready to deal with*
> *what happened to her?*

Okay, now I feel depressed.
"I don't know if I can ever
deal with what happened."

> *You have no choice, if you*
> *want to get well and stay*
> *that way. Can we talk*
> *about her now?*

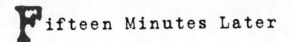ifteen Minutes Later

I've said all I'm going to
say about Mama, except,
"I can't remember her being
happy after Bryan was born.
I thought she should be happy—
he such a beautiful little
baby, no trouble at all, really.
But she was seriously depressed,
almost psychotic."

*That's not unusual for someone
with bipolar disorder, Vanessa.
Especially if that someone
was not being treated for
the condition. Had she been
diagnosed yet?*

"No. Not until Bryan started
kindergarten. It was actually
his teacher who pointed
out the symptoms to Grandma.
Gives you some idea of how
parent/teacher conferences went."

Dr. Starr smiles. *Yes, I can see that.*
You know, Vanessa, the stress
of pregnancy and the postpartum
period triggers depression
in a lot of women. If they have a
history of mental illness, they can
become dangerous. Was your mother
a danger to your brother or you?

What the hey? I've got
nothing to lose by telling
her and it might be good
to get it off my chest,
now that I don't have to worry
about Mama's fierce
brand of retribution.

I Said Mama Wasn't Happy

"But the truth is, she was
a total psycho some of the time.
When Bryan was a baby,
I was afraid to leave him
alone with Mama. One
time I came home from
school and he was screaming.
Mama had him in the kitchen
sink, giving him a bath.
The water was way too hot.
I yanked him from her hands,
his baby skin all red and steaming.

> *I have to scrub away his sin,*
> Mama said. *Jesus expects it.*

"A baby has no sin, Mama,"
I tried to tell her.

> *We are born into sin and must*
> *be cleansed. Damian says so.*

> Dr. Starr interrupts,
> *Who is Damian?*

"Mama's personal 'angel,'
who followed her everywhere.
I didn't think he was very
nice, for an angel."

*I see. Well, it was a good
thing you came in when
you did. Was that why you asked
your grandmother to step in?*

I nod. "That, and the fact
that Mama beat me
for 'arguing with the will
of the Lord.' I didn't think
much of the Lord for a very

long time."

Conner

Tomorrow We're Off

To the far distant side of
the Black Rock Desert, where the
mountains tumble down to crash-
land on the playa. Talk about

wilderness—rabbits, and
the coyotes who love them, that's
all we'll have for company except
each other and a watchdog or two.

Dr. Boston is worried
about me. *The Challenge is
not the place for heroics,
Conner. You'll be physically*

*tired and mentally drained
by the end of Day Five, no
matter how good the shape
you're in. You tend to want*

*to play savior. Promise me
you won't. Not out there, okay?*

"I appreciate that you're
worried, Dr. B. Don't be.

In fact, you've got me all
wrong. No savior complex
here. All I want is the key to
the front door. Adios. So long."

Her smile fades. *What then, Conner?
How will you deal with the kind
of pressure that brought you to
us? You cannot allow everyday*

*stress to make you put a gun
to your chest and pull the trigger.
I don't want to read in the paper
that my best patient has died.*

est?

"What do you mean by 'best'?
Least trouble? Cutest? Most
likely to succeed after he's
released? 'Cause I'm not that."

> *Why not, Conner? You were on*
> *a fast track to success. No*
> *reason to derail, is there?*
> *You've no lack of ambition.*

She gives me this great smile
and I wonder, for maybe
the thousandth time, what's
under her short little skirt.

I decide on the direct route.
"My main ambition, once
I leave here, is getting laid
by some gorgeous older woman. . . ."

> *I see*, says Dr. B (Heather?).
> *You know, we've never resolved*
> *this older woman thing. Can we*
> *possibly do that before you go?*

"Since I'm leaving tomorrow,
I suppose that means right now?"

> It does. Sometimes a feeling
> of attraction grows because
>
> a specific incident spurs it.
> You said your mother rarely
> touched you. Remember when you
> were small? Who did touch you?

I gasp beneath the weight
of memory, recollection
so evocative it dwarfs
all thought of Emily.

Eyes closed, I find her there
in the dark, hands like silk,
the kind you want to wear close
to your most private places.

492

Hands to Guide

Little boys to exactly those
places they want to see, to touch,
to taste. Perfect hands, that
flaunt her beauty. "Leona."

> *Your governess, the one who . . .*
> Heather halts midsentence,
> changes direction. *Can*
> *you talk about the assaults?*

I shake my head. "I never
thought about it that way.
Leona never assaulted me,
and the things she taught me

didn't hurt. I was always
expected to act all grown up.
She made me a man for real,
and no one suspected a thing."

> *No adult has the right to*
> *turn a child into a man,*
> *nor to teach him things*
> *he's too immature to learn.*

Leona was a predator, and
you were a willing victim—
a child in need of human warmth
can easily blur the line between

affection and perversion.
Your trust in Leona was not
deserved. She did assault you.
It just didn't hurt until now.

Too much to take in, too
much to purge. Why must
every memory, once sweet,
dead-end in such ugliness?

Too much . . .

Tony
Off We Go

On our grand adventure—
        most likely the only grand
adventure I'll ever have.
        Better make the most of
it—grab life by the scrotum
        and squeeze real hard.

We pile into a big Suburban,
        Sean behind the wheel and Raven
taking shotgun. Dahlia, Lori,
        and Justin grab the middle
seat, leaving the back to
        Conner, Vanessa, and me.

Just the way I like it. We head
        east from Reno, drive for miles
across vast, high desert.
                        Vanessa's knee rests against
                                mine. *You can see forever!*
                        It's beautiful, isn't it?

"Not as beautiful as you,"
        I say, loving the way
it makes her blush.

> *God, Tony,* says Lori, *if*
> > *I didn't know better, I'd*
> > *say you were playing her.*

Subtle as dreams, I reach
     for Vanessa's hand. "Nope,
not playing. Not at all."
                    Vanessa snakes her fingers
                         around mine, comfortable
                    with them there. *I know.*

I would expect Conner
     to say something, or at
least notice. But he just
     stares out the window, silent
as death. I wonder where he
     is right now, 'cause it's not here.

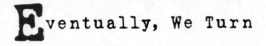

Eventually, We Turn

North off the interstate,
        onto a backwater highway.
To the east, the Black
        Rock Desert stretches
emptiness as far as the eye
        can take in. I've heard

it's an inferno come summer.
        But spring has softened it
with wildflowers and little
        creeks that fill big cracks
in the playa. I've never been
        here before, but I'll be back.

"Hey, Conner, you ever been
        to the Black Rock before?
Ever done Burning Man?"

                I have, interrupts Dahlia.
                    I went with my boyfriend
                last year. It was awesome.

Finally, Conner turns from
        the window. *You crazy?*
Getting naked, scarfing tofu,
        and chanting mantra for three
days with a bunch of dope-
        smoking pyromaniacs?

                        Dahlia laughs. *That about*
                                covers it, okay. It was
                        a total, out and out gas.
Conner notices Vanessa
        and me holding hands.
He scowls. *Whatever.*

"I always meant to check
        it out but never managed
to find a way out here," I
        say. "Hey, Vanessa, if I can
get us a ride, want to
        come with me this year?"

Before She Can Answer

Raven launches into
      a whole discussion
about the Burning Man
      Festival—how it started
as a fun Labor Day party,
      with campouts and bonfires.

How it has segued into
      a major assault on the
landscape, despite the best
      efforts of BLM officials
and every good intention of
      the partiers in question.

This desert may not look
      like it deserves respect,
she says. *But it is unique.*
      Fragile. And it is up to
us to protect it. I hope
      your time out here will

convince you of that.
        We are going to take
you places few people
            ever see. The journey
will not be easy. It will,
            as the name implies,

challenge you, in mind
            and body. But once
you complete it, I
            guarantee you will
come away with new
            respect for yourselves.

Respect for myself?
        The concept is totally
foreign. Improbable.
        If Challenge by Choice
can do that for me,
        I will always be

grateful.

Vanessa

We Stop for Lunch

In Gerlach, the last town
(if you could call it that)
before leaving civilization
completely. There's one gas
station, one post office, and
one restaurant—Bruno's.

We always stop here, says
Sean. *After this, it's MREs,
except for what we might
catch to eat fresh.*

"Catch? You mean like
bugs?" Images of gross-out
TV shows come to mind.

No, says Raven. *He means
like fish. Or maybe crawdads.
Ever try crayfish, fresh
from a mountain reservoir?*

"Eeeeuuuuu! Those little
lobster-looking things?
You actually eat those?"

Ask anyone in the Deep South,
they'll tell you they're heavenly,
Raven says. *And this time of year,*
they're hungry—easy to catch.

I decide I'd better eat every
crumb of this giant cheeseburger
and fries. It may be the last thing
I'll feel like eating for a while.
Sounds like we'll have some
serious choices to make.
Miniature shellfish. (You don't
eat the antennae, do you?)
Or just-add-water-to-refortify
meat, potatoes, and gravy.
Mmmm. I can hardly wait!

Back on the Road

And now it's a gravel road,
rutted and scarred by winter,
slow going in this old four-by.
Everyone seems subdued, lost
in daydreams, anxiousness,
or the hypnotic lull of the sameness
outside the windows. This is high
desert at its most monotonous—
the cracked, white playa, giving
way to miles and miles of sage,
greasewood, and cheatgrass.
And yet it's riveting, beautiful
in its starkness.

"Look." I point at deep impressions,
stamped in the playa.
"Wagon tracks. Can you believe
you can still see them? They're
more than a century old!"

          Beside me, Conner rouses.
          My great-great grandmother
          came to Nevada in one of those wagons.

He pauses, then finishes.
If she had stayed in Pennsylvania,
I wouldn't be here now.

It sounds more like a wish
than an observation, and it makes
me sad. "I'm glad you're here,
Conner. I don't know what
happened when you went home,
but you're not the same person
now. I miss the Conner who left."

He slides his arm around my
shoulder, pulls me close, whispers,
I'm sorry, Vanessa. You are
the most incredible girl I've ever
known, and you deserve much
better than me.

Okay, That Worries Me

Conner has always acted
completely self-assured,
in control. It's part of what
makes him so damn attractive.
I let my hand settle on his thigh,
wish we were somewhere
I could kiss him. Really
kiss him. "What's wrong,
Conner? Talk to me."

> He sags slightly, weighting
> the arm around my shoulder.
> *Do you know how great*
> *it would be to live a simple*
> *existence, like the pioneers*
> *did? Okay, I know they died*
> *from diseases we now kill*
> *with little pills. And I know*
> *life was tough without electricity*
> *and running water.*
>
> *But think, just think, how*
> *awesome it was not to worry*
> *about college, or an upwardly*
> *mobile career. No pressure,*

no expectations beyond staying
alive and keeping your family safe.
He covers my hand with his.
Think how people must have
loved each other when all
they had was each other.

That does sound nice, but life
wasn't really easy back then, not
that it's easier now. I'm still
not sure what's going on
in Conner's head. All I know
is I want to be inside there too.
So I tell him, very softly,
"We may have more than just
each other. But that doesn't
diminish what I feel

for you."

Conner

I Thought I Was Ready

To graduate Aspen Springs,
move ahead with my life.
I even quit taking the Prozac,
to prove to myself that I could.

I figured the Challenge would
provide enough stimulation
to let me go cold turkey.
Four days later I can't decide

if that's why I feel like I'm
fresh out of hope, or if it's
the big, ugly picture. Never
before did I doubt my ability

to one day leave Mom and Dad
in my dust, carve a niche, climb
inside and stay there, satisfied
with my personal pit of lust.

But my visit home only served
to implode all perception
of independence. The thing
with Emily showed how focused

my parents are on exerting
control indefinitely. Forever
is too long to spend, forced
into the "submissive" role.

And then Dr. Boston had to
dredge up all that stuff about
Leona. Talk about your
psychological sledgehammers.

She confronted me with a demon
I had buried a long time ago,
exhumed suppressed guilt
I had carried far too long.

And Now, Here's Vanessa

Offering abstract confessions
of affection. If I were
normal, how would I describe
our definite connection?

I love the way she feels in
the curve of my arm. I love
her unpretentious beauty,
her intelligence, her nerve.

But could I ever love *her*?
The concept of falling in love
is completely foreign, something
I can't bring myself to accept.

> Her hair pillows my cheek and
> her hand on my leg is warm.
> *I care about you, Conner,*
> *and I hate to see you hurting.*

I want to respond but can't
find the pretty words I need.

Tony comes to my rescue.
Do you two mind? I'm trying

to meditate here. Ohm. Ohm.
Damn! Now I'm distracted.

Once again I'm amazed at
how he can jump right in

and lighten even the heaviest
situation. Tony is gold.
More than probably anyone,
he has earned my admiration.

I know Vanessa loves him too.
"Why don't you join us?" I kid.
"I can't speak for Vanessa, but
I've always wanted to try

a threesome. Hetero only,
though. You up for that, Tony?"

I'll try anything once. And
you know, I just might like it.

We Stop to Stretch Our Legs

And take a piss in the desert.
Not difficult for the guys,
but embarrassing for the ladies.
The result is a lecture on

> wilderness hygiene, delivered
> with great panache by Raven.
> *Please spread out to urinate,
> and if you must defecate,*
>
> *grab this little shovel and be
> sure to dig at least a foot
> deep. You do not want to leave
> your shit where lions can find it.*

Dahlia is impressed. *Lions?*
What do you mean, lions?

> Raven clarifies. *Mountain lions—
> plentiful here, but rarely seen,*
>
> *because generally they would
> rather not mess with people.
> Still, the odd cat can have a taste
> for humans, so let me stress*

the importance of knowing how
to deal with a cat if you happen
on one. Don't run. Make noise. Fight
back. Don't look like an easy meal.

Dahlia looks like cougar fast
food—a no-brain meal. *I can't*
believe I might have to fight
a lion. That's totally screwed.

Tony jabs, *No worries, dear.*
A cat would take one bite and spit
you back out. You're tasteless. Now,
if you'll excuse me, I have to make

a pit stop.

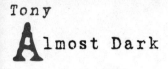

Tony
Almost Dark

We bump up beside a rock
        outcropping, get ready
to camp for the night.

        How many of you have
                camped in the wilderness
        before? asks Sean.

"Define wilderness," I say.
        "Does it include the parks
and alleys in Reno?"

        Sean cracks half a smile.
                That's a different kind
        of wilderness, Tony.

"Tell me about it. It smells
        a whole lot better out
here in the boonies."

        We want to leave it that
                way. You already know about
        how to relieve yourselves. . . .

Sean launches into a whole
                "leave no tracks" routine,
even though we've already
                been over it in our orientation:
*Carry in, carry out; don't
                disturb wildlife or vegetation.* . . .

Bored immediately, I turn
                my attention to Raven, who's
unloading gear. Some of it
                looks pretty heavy. Hope
we don't have to carry *that*
                stuff in or out, but something

tells me we do. I spy a
                steep trail, leading up
into the mountains.
                No way a vehicle would
manage that. Looks like
                we'll be walking from here.

Raven Shows Us

How to build a portable
          shelter—four poles and
a canvas roof, no walls.
          Then she gives each of us
a backpack, a thin sleeping
          bag, and barely enough

clothes to get us through
          three reeking weeks.
We arrange our sleeping
          bags, boys on one side
of the newly built fire pit,
          girls on the other, and

suddenly I notice how
          cold it becomes, once
the sun takes a dive.

                    Better gather some fire-
                              wood, Sean says, *before*
                    it gets much darker.

We all spread out, looking
          for something that qualifies.
Mostly, it's sage twigs.

Sage burns hot and fast.
            Better get plenty, Raven warns.
It's going to be a cold one.

Raven lights the fire, and
        just about then I notice
there are no lanterns.

            No cookstoves, either, she
                        says. *Did you expect*
            a Coleman display?

            All that stuff is heavy,
                        not what you'll want
            to be carrying in your
                        packs over miles of
            rough territory, let
                        alone up a rock cliff.

Things Swim into Focus

For some stupid reason
       I had it in mind that we'd
do a little hiking, a little
       climbing, then return
to our neat little camp for
       dinner and bedtime stories.

Looks like tonight is
       the closest we'll get,
and we're already miles
       from anything I pictured.
The others look nervous
       too. Except for Conner.

Since we had a big lunch,
       says Raven, *we'll skip*
MREs tonight, and stick
       with fresh veggies and fruit.
Even if you don't really like
       them, you'll miss them soon.

She breaks out apples,
        bananas, grapes, raw
carrots, and broccoli,
        plus an assortment of
crackers and cheeses.
        You'll miss cheese, too.

I already miss hot food,
        which is strange. I've
gone for days with nothing
        more than stale bread and
peanut butter. Spoiled
        by Aspen Springs?

Groans and crunching
        noises fill the cool air
inside our temporary
        shelter. We all gather
around the fire, not quite
        getting warm. Everyone,

except Conner.

Vanessa

Okay, This Is Less

Than I bargained for—primitive,
not to mention cold.
Even around the campfire,
our breath puffs
into the evening air, mixing
with smoke as if we're all
indulging a nicotine habit.
No bad habits out here,
except for our meds,
dutifully distributed
by Raven the Taskmistress.

We sit shoulder-to-shoulder
in silence, trying to snatch
a little body warmth, as
the meds kick in.
Only Conner sits off to one
side, not affected by
temperature, but surely bothered
by something. Despite all
the ice-breaking on the way
here, he's frozen solid.

One thing I notice, since I can
hardly keep my eyes off him,
is how he waits for Raven
to turn her back before spitting
out the pill she hands him.
Softly, he digs a little hole
in the sand with one hiking
boot, slips the med inside,
smoothes it over, buried treasure.

My eyes travel to Tony,
and I see he is watching
Conner too. Finally he glances
at me, and we offer a mutual shrug.

He scoots closer. *Don't worry,*
Vanessa. Everything will be okay.
Conner knows what he's doing.

I Wander into the Sage

For a pre-bed pee, notice how
the stars have assaulted the black
of night sky. The moon is on slow
rise, and I'm sure I have never
witnessed anything so stunning.
My flashlight illuminates
a path, worn through the vegetation,
and I choose it as the easy way
before wondering about what
made the trail to begin with.

As I squat down behind a taller
bush, hoping my silhouette won't
be seen from the campfire,
movement in the brush startles
me into rising, pants dropped.
I wave my flashlight, left
to right, and I find myself
eyeball-to-eyeball with a deer,
not four feet away. I see no
antlers, so it must be a doe,
as scared of me as I was
of her just a few seconds ago.

"It's okay, pretty thing," I say,
real quiet so I don't make her
even more scared.
But with a flick of her tail,
she dashes away, into
the safety of the night.

Vanessa? Where are you?
calls Raven, traipsing through
the sage, hot on my trail, as
if taking off, sixty-some miles
to the nearest approximation
of civilization, were an option.

I yank up my pants. "Over
here." Trading heartbeats
with a deer. "I'm coming.
It's freezing out here."

Scrunched Down Into

The relative warmth of our
sleeping bags, we listen to Sean,
outlining tomorrow's goals:

*We leave the truck here, head
up into the hills. The higher we
go, the more likely it is we'll
run into snow, so the going
may get muddy. Try to avoid
slushy puddles. If your feet
get wet, you're going to blister,
and we won't slow down for
that—or anything that can
be avoided, with a little
common sense.*

Raven adds, *This isn't
TV. You may have watched*
Survivor *or that show called*
Brat Camp. *Hard as those
may look, the camera guys
following everyone around
mitigate real hardship.*

We're not here to hurt you,
but we're not going to help
in situations you create,
or those you can dig
yourselves out of.

Back to Sean. *There will be*
times when you'll have to
resort to teamwork to accomplish
a leg of the program. Working
together is how you'll get
through the Challenge, and how
you'll get through life.

Trying to find sleep, I look
out at the stars, and just as I
start to settle down, a coyote

starts to sing.

Conner

Coyote Booty Calls

Crack the night's smooth silence,
raising quiet alarm among
the ranks. "Relax, everyone.
A coyote's diet is pretty

much rabbits, mice, and the
occasional cat. And if you're
concerned about rabies, worry
more about the stray bat who

happens into our shelter."
God, it's great to watch them
squirm, every eye straining
to find an odd winged creature,

flapping beneath the canopy.
Yip, yip, yip invites one scruffy
excuse for a canine. I hear
a sleeping bag zip tighter.

> At my right, Tony laughs.
> *Relax, Justin. You know*
> *Jesus won't let those coyot's*
> *make midnight snacks out of us.*

Justin answers, *Jesus helps
those who help themselves, but I
wouldn't expect someone like
you to know things like that.*

*What do you mean, "someone like
me?" I hope that's not an attack
on my character. Because that is
not a Christian philosophy.*

Wisely, Justin crawls back into
his pit of surly silence.

Quiet down now, orders Sean.
You'll be getting up early.

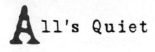All's Quiet

Except for the chorus of
medicated snores, and I
half-regret not joining
them in sedated limbo.

Instead I'm lying here, on
a hard crust of playa sand,
listening to the desert night,
inhaling sage-scented dust,

blown up by a bone-chilling
wind. Seems you don't notice
the cold, cradled by downers,
mired in Valium dreams.

Cold or no, I will stick to
my decision to rid my body
of drugs while I'm out here—
supervision-free detox.

No more a.m. stimulants, p.m.
depressants, which might appeal
to a very large crowd of loser
adolescents. But not me.

Mom and Dad would be proud—
Yeah, right. Who am I kidding?
After all the trauma, all
the drama, I'll never quite

make their greatest achievements
list. Something cheerful to think about,
brain fighting my body's request
for sleep. Through a heavy mist

of exhaustion comes a blitz
of memories—Dr. Boston,
Leona, Emily, all women
I tried my best to please

in whatever ways they asked.
And I see that it was all just
a warped bid for attention
from one woman—Mommy.

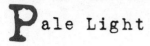ale Light

Filters through my closed
eyelids, pierces my pupils,
rouses me into morning,
forbids any hope of sleep.

> *Rise and shine, happy campers!*
> croaks Sean. *Coffee's brewing.*
> *What the fuck, asshole?* responds
> Dahlia. *What time is it? Like dawn?*

> *It's time to haul your lazy*
> *butt out of the sack!* says Raven.
> Dahlia groans. *Fine. I'm hauling.*
> *But don't expect peak performance.*

No worries. No one would ever
expect peak performance from
you. Tony's jab draws tired laughter.
Not that we don't all respect you.

> Sean orders, *Okay, everyone*
> *pay attention. The morning*
> *routine goes like this: up at*
> *daybreak, sleeping bags rolled*

up and stashed in your backpacks,
ten minutes for bodily functions
(please go in separate directions),
breakfast, teeth, and then off we go.

I drag myself out of my cocoon,
roll it up tightly as I can manage,
then reach for a cup of coffee to
fight the black hole of sleeplessness

I have pushed myself into.
I hope Sean and Raven will
take it easy on us the first
day. I doubt I can cope with

a marathon.

Tony

After a Scrumptious Breakfast

(Egg McMuffin–flavored
            substance, in a foil pouch),
Raven and Sean start
            handing us things to stow
in our packs, on top of
            our already wrinkled clothes.

Rope. More foil pouches.
            (Guess we have to carry
our own gourmet goop.)
            One roll of toilet paper
each. (Guess MREs don't
            make for megadumps.

Hope they've got laxatives
            along!) Antibacterial
soap. (For hair and skin,
            safe for the environment.)
Flint and steel. Fire-starter
            tinder. (We're trusting *this*?)

Featherlight thermal
          blankets. (Thank you,
NASA.) Pocket hand
          warmers. (Where are
we going, anyway? To
          the Antarctic?) Lip ice.

Mosquito repellent. Sunglasses.
          (Awesome idea.
The glare out here is
          killer. Sure glad someone's
got the system down.)
          A minifishing kit, with one

hook, one bobber, one sinker,
          and a small reel of line.
(Hope Phillip's watching
          this. If so, he's smiling.)
"Hey, Phillip," I whisper.
          "Are you there, somewhere?"

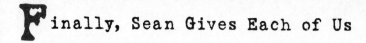

Finally, Sean Gives Each of Us

A whistle on a long red
          cord, just right to go
around our necks and
          hang in easy reach.
Three short blasts
          means you're in trouble.

Everyone has to give
          theirs a try. The noise
scatters a warren of jackrabbits,
          out on a scouting
expedition. What do rabbits
          eat out here, anyway? Sand?

Before we head out,
          we're going to buddy
up, Raven says. Always
          keep your buddy in sight,
or at least know where
          he or she is at all times.

Raven assigns partners,
        choosing Lori for hers.
Vanessa and Dahlia.
        Justin and Sean. Which
leaves Conner and me.
        A week ago I would

have been fine with that,
        ecstatic, in fact. But this
thing with Conner eighty-sixing
        his meds has me worried.
He buried his Prozac again
        this morning. I know

quitting cold isn't always
        a problem, but it can be.
What if he drops off
        the deep end? "How
responsible for our
        partners are we?" I ask.

Conner Shoots a Curious Look

In my direction. Hell,
      maybe he's worried
about looking out for me.

               Good question, replies
                    Sean. *And the answer*
               is: ninety-nine percent.

"What about the one
          percent? Can you be
more specific, please?"

               I can. If your buddy
                    decides to run off into
               the night, don't go too.

          Everyone takes a minute
               or two to digest the buddy
          system thing. Now, Q & A:

               Q: *What if my buddy breaks a leg?*
          A: *Blow your whistle. We'll*
               triage on site, call for help.

Q: *What if she won't participate?*
       A: *Encourage her. Get in her*
face *if you have to.*
              Q: *What if that doesn't work?*
A: *Blow one long blast on*
              your whistle; leave it to us.

My turn. "And what
       if your buddy flips
out completely?"

                     Sean looks at Conner,
                            looks back at me. *Is*
                     that really a concern?

I turn toward Conner,
       assess the dark circles
around his sleep-deprived
       eyes. He smiles a very
strange smile and gives a
       little shrug, and I say,

"Guess not."

Vanessa

Buddies with Dahlia

Wonderful. She and I have
probably exchanged
a hundred words in
the last fifteen weeks.
But hey, I guess
that's the point.
Challenge by Choice—
the way to form lasting (?)
friendships. I decide to break
the ice. "Are you into hiking?"

> *You kidding? Most hiking*
> *I've ever done is from*
> *my house down to*
> *the corner 7-Eleven.*
> *What about you?*

"I've been a few times,
with my grandma. She's in
pretty good shape for her age.
She likes to hike Mt. Rose
Meadows, and we did part
of the Rim Trail, too."

Holy crap! She must be
in pretty good shape.
Is she old, or what? 'Cause
my grandma is older than dirt.

I shrug. "Almost sixty.
But she always seemed
younger to me than
my mom did. My mom
was born ancient."

Your mom is the crazy
one, right? Straight
to the point.

So I'll give a direct
answer. "She was."

Before I Have to Offer Details

Raven rounds us up.
Okay, everyone ready?
Today's leg isn't really
difficult. It's more to assess
what shape you're in
than to really challenge you.
Our goal is ten miles
before nightfall.

Ten miles isn't difficult?
I've never walked more
than five at any one time
with Grandma. But I guess
I'm up to the task.
Raven and Lori take the lead
as we start up a gradual grade
on a wide, well-maintained trail.

Keep a nice, steady pace
and watch your posture,
or your backs will curse
you. Don't overcompensate
for the weight of your packs,
Raven instructs.

Right about now, I start
to feel the weight of my
pack. Immediately, I want
to compensate—a major
trick of the mind?
I glance to my right,
see Dahlia is fighting
the same urge. "Wonder
how long it takes before
our backs start swearing."

> *I woke up this morning and my*
> *back was already cussing big-time,*
> Dahlia replies. *If you can't hear*
> *it, you need a hearing aid!*

Two Hours Later

My back is cussing too.
In fact, with all the spinal
swearing going on, you almost
can't hear the moans
and groans of our feet.

> Finally Raven directs
> us off the trail, into a little
> clearing in the sage. *We'll
> take a breather here.
> Everyone drink water,
> even if you don't think
> you're thirsty. Believe
> me, you are, and staying
> hydrated is vital.*

Water never tasted near
this good before. I polish
off a bottle, realize I can't
just toss the empty.

> *Hang on to those bottles,*
> says Sean. *We'll refill them
> when we get to the creek.
> Anyone hungry? Tough!
> Lunch isn't for an hour.
> Backpacks up. Let's go.*

Sean and Justin trade
places with Raven and Lori.
Conner and Tony move
behind them, in front
of Dahlia and me.

As Tony passes, he touches
my arm. *You okay? 'Cause
I'm one sore puppy already.*

"Woof, woof," I joke.
But right now it doesn't seem

too funny.

Conner

We've Been Walking

For three days, uphill, loaded
with heavy packs. Oxen.
That's what we are, just like
those whose time-smoothed tracks

we follow. I keep wondering
if we're going somewhere, or
just wandering at random, not
even Sean knowing our final

destination. The weather
is typical spring in northern
Nevada—tepid during the day,
and that's a very good thing.

Hiking these hills in the heat
of July would be insane.
So far the grade isn't bad,
the trail well marked and dry.

But we haven't covered near
the distance Sean and Raven
expected to, mostly due to
Lori's insistence that she

"can't take another step." That's
bull, of course, but her less-than-
adequate speed has kept us from
taking full advantage of

the relatively easy terrain.
Things only get harder from
here—steeper, more slippery—
so unless the bitch grows wings

our progress will slow even
more. Not sure why it matters,
especially if wandering at
random actually *is* the score.

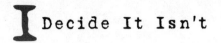

I Decide It Isn't

Because as we set up camp for
the night, I hear Raven and Sean
discussing tomorrow. Seems
our first real test is in sight.

> *So what do you think? Are they*
> *all up to the gorge?* asks Raven.
>> *Guess we'll find out,* answers Sean.
>> *Anyway, we haven't had a fall yet.*

> *I'm a little worried about*
> *Lori. She's not exactly fit.*
>> *She will pose a challenge,*
>> *but hey, no guts, no glory.*

> *"Glory" is not in her dictionary.*
> *I hope "vertigo" isn't either.*
>> *She's your buddy, sweetheart.*
>> *Just show her the rope-a-dope.*

Should be an interesting
day. I'll be sure to let Lori
and Raven go first. That
way I won't miss a thing.

I unroll my sleeping bag,
smoothing the sand beneath
best I can, wishing the stone-
free surface was soothing

enough to actually let me
sleep. Four nights without
drifting all the way off into
deep REM refreshment

has left me disoriented.
So far only Tony has
a clue, but with my thought
processes bordering on bizarre,

that's likely to change any
time. Maybe exhaustion will
conquer my brain tonight, beat
it into sublime submission.

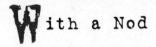
With a Nod

Toward early homo erectus,
Tony lights this evening's
fire, using only flint and steel.
Around bites of pepperoni paste

>   he asks, *How did humans*
>   *ever survive? I mean,*
>   *people consider themselves*
>   *so clever, but really,*
>
>   *learning to light a fire like*
>   *this had to be an accident,*
>   *or a direct communication*
>   *from our Great Dad Above.*

>   Sitting close to the blossoming
>   fire, Justin squirms visibly.
>   *I wish you wouldn't use*
>   *terms like "Great Dad Above."*

Tony smiles. *Why not? Do*
you really think He cares
about terminology? I bet He
worries more about how few

of His greatest experiments
believe He exists. With just
that mustard seed of faith, think
what people might achieve.

"Faith is for little children
and giant fools. Don't tell
me you believe in Santa, too!"
Defiant, I hardly slur at all.

Tony grins. *Of course, and*
the Tooth Fairy, too. All fairies,
in fact. Then he grows serious.
I'm sorry you're afraid of truth.

Me too.

Tony

I Am Firestarter

And I feel powerful.
        Strange, because I
never felt that way
        lighting a match,
which really is an
        awesome invention.

But conquering flint and
        steel gives me a kind
of primal satisfaction.
        So far only Conner,
Dahlia, and I have
        figured out how to do it.

                Vanessa comes over,
                        gives me a high five.
                Way to go, Tony. If
                        I ever decide to go
                camping again, I'll
                        invite you to come.

"Promise? Maybe we
         could bring along
a sleeping bag for two.
         It would have to be
a whole lot warmer than
         these half-ass units."

                    No doubt about that.
                         She sits beside me,
                real close, and for about
                         the thousandth time,
                I'm amazed at how
                         she makes me feel.

As inconspicuously
         as possible, I slide
my arm around her
         waist, put my mouth
against her ear. "I don't
         ever want to lose you."

Losing Her

Would snuff the light
        out of my life—a light
I never believed I
        could find again after
Phillip died. Yet here it
        is, sitting right next to me.

Shit. Damn. Fuck.
        On the far side of
the flames, Dahlia
        is working her hiking
boots off swollen feet.
        Check out this blister!

Raven moves into
        paramedic mode,
rushing to Dahlia's
        side as if she's having
a baby or something.
        She pokes and prods.

It's ugly, all right.
> *Vanessa, get the first*
aid kit. First, we need
> *some rubbing alcohol.*
Okay, this is going
> *to hurt a little. . . .*

Quit screaming. It
> *can't hurt that bad!*
Now, use this
> *ointment. Dab it*
all over the blister,
> *then leave it exposed.*

> Dahlia keeps yelling.
>> *You want me to go*
> *barefoot? I'll freeze.*
A blister like that needs
> *air. Later we'll fix you*
up with a moleskin.

Dahlia Bitches Until Bedtime

I could kick her ass,
        but not because she's
causing a major scene
        over a minor problem,
making a mountain (ha-
        ha) out of a moleskin.

No, I'd like to wring
        her scrawny neck for
taking Vanessa from
        my side to go play
nurse's aide. I can still
        feel the warmth of her.

I settle into my sleeping
        bag, wondering at this
change that has come
        over me. Not only do
I love Vanessa, I think
        I want to make love to her.

Next to me, as if reading
            my mind, Conner says,
You're really in love with
            her, aren't you? Do you
want to be with her . . . I
            mean . . . you know?

I keep my voice very
        low. "I'm really in
love with her, yes.
        She makes me feel
like no one ever has.
        As for the rest, maybe."

                I think you should. You
                        told me once you weren't
                really sure who you are.
                        Being with Vanessa
                might answer that
                        question for you.

It just might.

Vanessa

It's All So Weird

How things are turning out.
A month ago I was hot
after Conner. And he wanted
me, I know he did.
But that has all grown
very cool, and it's not
because of the weather.
I mean, I still love him.
But it's not the "hot for his bod"
love I felt before, and now
I want to save him.
Why do I think
Mr. Exceptional needs saving?

A month ago I thought Tony
needed saving. But I don't think
so now. And now, God help
me, I'm pretty sure
I'm in love with Tony.
Not only that, but I'm very sure
he's in love with me.
Grandma once told me
it's easy to overthink love,
to dissect and question it
until it is no more.

I'm trying very hard not
to do that at this moment.
But the night holds
many questions.

On the far side of the shelter,
Conner and Tony are
whispering, and I get
the definite feeling
they're whispering
about me. I'd like to
crawl over, burrow
between them, fall asleep
listening to them
whisper about me.

Up at Dawn

I grab the little shovel
and my roll of biodegradable
t.p. and head out into the brush,
hoping for some private
time before everyone else
gets up and notices
where I've gone. Talk
about embarrassing! Privacy
is hard to come by, with
everyone in such close
proximity to everyone else.

As the sun creeps higher,
the sky goes from gray
to vicious blue. Cold.
Clear. Perfect blue.
And it hits me that blue has never
seemed so beautiful.
And it hits me even harder
that I have not felt so good—so
well—in a long, long time.
I've only thought about steel—
sharp and real—once or twice
in the last few days.

When I get back to camp,
Tony finds me. *Morning.*
Conner says we're facing
some major challenge today.

"Other than Dahlia
griping about her feet?"

Much bigger than that,
although the blister may
make it even more
challenging for her, I guess.

"So what is this major
challenge? Walking a tight-
rope across the Grand Canyon?"

The Grand Canyon is in
Arizona. But you're close.

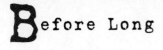efore Long

Sean lays out all the details
of our first real test.
*Today we're going to have
some fun, crossing this little
ol' canyon on a rope bridge.
It's not so difficult, unless
you happen to have
a problem with heights.*

I don't *think* I have
a problem with heights.
Still, "How high is 'high'?"

*Around a hundred
and fifty feet, says Raven.
Think of a fifteen-story
building, and you're close.*

"And how far across
do we have to go?"

*Thirty yards. Not
so far, really. But you
do need to understand
the technique.*

Fifteen minutes later
we have a basic idea
of how to cross a gorge
on a network of ropes,
strung at least a decade
ago by a bunch of Boy Scouts.
I sure hope they earned
their merit badges that day!
(You do have to do things
right to get a merit badge,
don't you?) I also hope they
used rope with a minimum
ten-year warranty.
As we pack up and head
out, a sensuous shiver
of fear works its way

up my spine.

Conner
Four Miles

To the gorge, we hike single
file. The buzz is constant.

> Dahlia: *My blister is killing*
> *me. I have to sit down awhile.*

> Tony: *I wish that damn blister*
> *would hurry and finish you off.*
> Justin: *If I were you, Dahlia,*
> *I'd worry about infection.*

> Lori: *Jeez, Justin, don't tell her*
> *that. She'll bitch and moan all day.*
> Vanessa: *Ain't that the truth?*
> *Guess we'll just have to ditch her.*

Just after lunch, we crest
a small rise, and there in
the scrub is a band of mustangs.
The stallion snorts in surprise,

but for a short moment we
all freeze, humans checking
out horses and vice versa.
Then Lori happens to sneeze.

With a flick of his black tail,
the stallion raises an alarm
and charges off to the east,
trailed by a battalion of mares.

        Dahlia forgets her blister.
        Oh! My! God! Did you see that?
Tony delivers his usual
banter. *No, D, we're all blind.*

        Vanessa scoots up beside him.
        Weren't they just gorgeous?
Not nearly as gorgeous as you,
Tony answers. *But close, okay.*

We Reach a Place

Where winter runoff has carved
a fast stream through the rock.
It plunges down the mountain
with a huge blast of noise.

Over the creek, not very high,
is a rope contraption, maybe
ten feet across and flimsy.
Do they really call this a "bridge?"

It consists of a single thick
cable to walk on and two chest
high "sides" made of crisscrossed
ropes. It looks totally unstable!

Sean doesn't give us a chance
to think about it too long.
*The trick to crossing is keeping
your hands and feet in sync.*

*Point your toes to the side,
walk on the arches of your
feet. Reach with your hands,
move your feet, try not to rock*

from side to side or you'll
lose your balance. If you keep
your eyes straight ahead and
use common sense, you'll be fine.

Sean demonstrates the proper
technique, crossing easily.
Okay, who's going first? Come
on. We don't have all week.

We glance back and forth
among us, no one especially
wanting to step up to the plate.
I'm not real keen on it myself,

but what the hell? "I'm game."
Safety first, Raven decks me
out with a harness and helmet.
What's the worst that could happen?

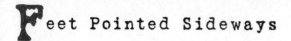eet Pointed Sideways

Walking on my arches, eyes
straight ahead, I find a good
hand/foot rhythm. Even so,
once or twice I shift my weight

too quickly, making the ropes
creak and sway. A wave of
vertigo descends. I feel
nauseous. Weary. Weak.

*Keep going, Conner. You're
doing great*, encourages Sean.

Water rushes beneath me,
spewing foam. I want to

spew too, but that would
necessitate moving. "I can't."

*Sure you can. You're almost
there now. It's a straight shot.*

A gush of anger engulfs
my brain. For some reason,
I want to grab the guy by
the throat, squeeze, cause him pain.

Not sure why I feel that way,
but for whatever reason,
it puts my feet in motion—slow
motion, over the water's roar.

Everyone cheers, including
Sean, so I guess I won't choke
him just yet. Anyway, with my
success, the anger has vanished.

One by one, the others cross
without serious incident.
No one says a word about
my moment of doubt, except

Tony.

Tony

Never Thought I'd See

Conner look so scared.
     He's always completely
in control—of himself
     and everyone else. But he
just about lost it back
     there. I swear, he looked

like death. No one wants
     to talk to him about it,
but someone really should,
     and seeing as how I'm
his designated buddy, I
     guess that someone is me.

"Hey, man. You okay?
     Jeez, I thought I was
going to have to rescue
     you, and I'm pretty
damn sure that was
     not a rope for two."

I expect a witty comeback.
　　　　Instead, he says, *I'm not*
sure what happened.
　　　　It isn't like I've ever been
bothered by heights.
　　　　But I got really dizzy.

I've got a pretty good
　　　　idea what's to blame.
Just don't know if I
　　　　should say something.
On the other hand, we
　　　　have a more daunting

challenge, just ahead.
　　　　"You haven't really
slept so well lately,
　　　　have you? I mean,
since you've been
　　　　off your meds."

Now I Expect Denial

But I don't get that,
            either. *I had to quit*
them, Tony. They made
            me feel like a total
loser geek. "Up" all day,
            drop down at night,

until I wasn't sure just
            where I was supposed
to be anymore. How
            can I ever feel normal,
propped up (or down)
            by pharmaceuticals?

In a way, I have to
            agree. "I know what
you mean. Someday
            I'll have to quit them
too. But was this really
            the best time to do it?"

In hindsight, probably
          not. But I made my
decision, and I plan
          to stick to it. It will
either kill me or heal me.
          Let's hope for the latter.

As we start off again, I'm
          more worried than ever
about Conner. Part of me
          screams that I should tell
Sean or Raven, rat him
          out for his own good.

Another part insists I
          should keep my big
mouth shut. It should
          be Conner's decision,
as long as he isn't in
          danger. He isn't, is he?

We Hike for Another Hour

And now we're facing
         the gorge—a huge chasm
between two stone walls,
         over a hundred feet high,
and we're standing
         at the top of one of them.

To get to the top of the
         other one, we'll have
to cross via a rope bridge.
         It's a lot more substantial
than the macrame across the
         creek. This one has two

narrow boards for our
         feet. But if it happens
to swing, I suspect
         we'll all feel about like
Conner did, stuck out in
         the middle, nothing

but air beneath our
        feet. Speaking of
Conner, he looks okay
        for the moment, stable,
if just a little pale.
        "You cool, Conner?"

                        I'll be okay. And hey,
                                if I get stuck halfway,
                        refuse to go farther,
                                do me a favor and give
                        me a push, okay? Not
                                forward. Over the side.

At least his sense
        of humor is back.
"You got it, buddy.
        Over the side it is."
Still worried, I barely
        listen to Raven, giving

us instructions.

Vanessa

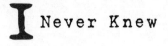

I Never Knew

I was tentative about heights.
Of course, I've never really
put myself to this kind of test
before. Hiking the Rim Trail,
we were up high, but there
was plenty of ground
beneath our feet.
Nothing under us here
but a long way down.

> *No way you can fall,*
> Raven tells us. *You'll be*
> *in safety harnesses, tied*
> *off to Sean or me. The main*
> *thing to remember is to keep*
> *moving. Stop in the middle*
> *and look down, things*
> *might get dicey. Okay,*
> *once again, who's first?*

This time it isn't Conner
who volunteers. (And what
was up with *him*, anyway?)

This time, Lori steps
to the front of the line.
*I'll go. Always good to get
these things over with.*

          Raven helps her shrug
          into a harness as Sean
          crosses to the other side.
          Slowly. One foot in front
          of the next. No problem.
          Do it just like that, Raven
          says. *Ready? Go for it.*

Cautiously, head high,
eyes straight ahead,
Lori does exactly like
Sean did, crossing
without hesitation.
Across the gorge, she
turns and yells, *Awesome!*

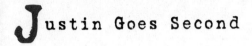

Justin Goes Second

           And as we watch, Tony
           comes up to me. *You good*
           with this? Doesn't look
           too awful. Of course,
           Conner would tell me my
           false sense of security is
           due to too many drugs.

"Could be. So can I have
some? Oops. Slip of the tongue.
What I meant was, can
I have some drugs?"

           Tony laughs. *Feel free to*
           slip your tongue any time,
           long as you slip it my way.
           But seriously, you feel
           okay about doing this?

Justin has reached the other
side. He turns, grinning,
and waves. "If he can do it,
I can do it." I lower my voice.
"But what about Conner?"

He says he's fine, that he
just felt a little queasy
for a second or two. He also
said if he stops halfway
one of us should push
him over the side.
He was at least half joking.

A crack in his rock.
solid armor? "I figured
he'd be the first one to
master every challenge
out here. Do you really
think he's okay?"

Tony turns to look at Conner,
standing off alone—his new MO.
No, Vanessa, he says.
I don't think so at all.

As If to Prove Him Wrong

Conner strides over to Raven,
climbs into a harness
and, without a single misstep,
handles the gorge
like it was nothing
more than a drainage ditch.
"Okay then. Guess
I'll go next."

> Tony lays a hand on
> my shoulder. *Vanessa?*
> *Just in case you or I don't*
> *make it . . .* He grins, then
> leans his face toward mine,
> *. . . please remember this.*
> His lips, chapped and cold,
> find mine. His kiss is sweet,
> filled with emotion. *Love you.*

I expect repercussions—
a warning from Raven,
a catcall from Dahlia.
But either no one noticed
or no one cared.
"I love you, too, Tony.
Now wish me luck."

The harness is heavier
than I thought it would be—
it makes me feel fairly
secure. At least I'm pretty
sure I won't end up at
the bottom of the gorge,
no matter what the bridge does.

As she helps me into it,
Raven says, *You and Tony
getting serious? I had
a different idea about
him, you know.*

"Yeah, I know. So did I,

once."

Conner
Feeling Pumped Tonight

All of us are. Conquering
the gorge was exhilarating.
For me, it was necessary.
Proving I could forge across

without flinching means just
about everything at the moment.
Tonight, I really believe
I can make it without meds.

After a delicious meal of pot
roast mush, we break into little
groups. Justin and Sean go off
to talk about life, post-Challenge.

Raven joins Dahlia and Lori's
conversation about safe sex,
and if there's any such thing
(other than masturbation).

Interesting, I guess, but not
the right group for me. For
once on this trip, I don't want
to spend the night sitting alone.

Which leaves Tony and Vanessa.
"Mind if I sit with you two?"

> *Thought you'd never ask*, says Tony.
> *You've been kind of antisocial.*

> Vanessa chides, *Leave him*
> *alone or he'll go away!*

"I guess I have been sulky.
I'm prone to that, you know."

> *If we didn't know it before,*
> *we sure do now.* Tony smiles.
> *Anyway, we were just discussing*
> *your poor cure for acrophobia.*

It Takes a Minute

To catch his drift. "Oh, you mean
heaving me over the side?
It was a much better option
than leaving me hanging there."

> *Probably right,* agrees Tony.
> *Think how nasty you would have
> been by the time we headed
> back. Bet you'd really stink.*

"In case you haven't noticed,
I don't smell very damn good
right now." The whole truth, and
nothing but. Oh frigging well.

> *I think you smell like roses,*
> Tony jokes. *Decomposing
> roses, that is, like a perfumed
> bathroom at an old folks' home.*

> *G-ross!* Vanessa wrinkles up
> her nose. *And anyway, just how
> would you know how that smells?
> You ever been in one of those?*

Not exactly. Tony grows serious.
But I've spent time with someone
fading toward death—held his
hand, inhaled the scent of living

flesh as it rots away. An old
folks' home must smell the same,
and no air freshener could
disguise that odor. It chokes

you, gags you, but you have
to pretend that you're doing
just fine, not trembling with
fear because the end is close.

You can feel death hovering,
waiting for his very last
breath, his final shudder;
anticipating taking him away.

He's Talking About Phillip

Vanessa and I remain silent
until Tony stops talking,
quiets completely. A sudden
chill massages my spine. Ghosts?

Ghosts, spirits, or just unfocused
me, suddenly I want to know
more about Phillip—what,
exactly, he meant to Tony.

"I'm sorry you lost Phillip,"
I try. "Tell me more about
him. Were the two of you
in love?" Tony wants to cry.

But he doesn't. *I loved*
Phillip, yes, and he loved
me. But we weren't in love,
not the way you might guess.

We met in the park. He was
out for a walk and I was
panhandling strangers, bumming
change, hoping for a score,

even if that meant offering up
my body. Phillip rescued me,
took me home, took me in, but
never tried to have sex with me.

He treated me like a son—
his own son wouldn't talk to
his old gay dad—and I let him
be the father I'd never known.

Phillip had AIDS and didn't want
to die alone. You might think
that's selfish, but he gave the world
to me and I will always

cherish him.

Tony

No Sex with Phillip

Is that what Conner
            wanted to hear? How
about Vanessa? Did she
            wonder about that too?
Probably, and I guess
            it might have been

a fair assumption,
            considering everyone
(except maybe Vanessa)
            thinks I'm totally gay.
"So are you surprised that
            I didn't sleep with Phillip?"

                Conner is slow to answer,
                        but Vanessa speaks
                right up. *Not really.*
                        I guess the thought
                might have crossed my
                        mind, but it didn't matter.

I admire your friendship
          with Phillip. I never had
a friend that I cared so
          much about. Not, at least,
until I met you. I wish
          I could have met him.

"I wish you could have
          too. He would have
loved you, almost as
          much as I do." At this
moment, my love for her
          is almost overwhelming.

          Finally Conner says,
                    pointedly, *I'm confused.*
          Are you gay? Bi? In
                    between? Do you want to
          have sex with Vanessa
                    or just be her friend?

I Have to Admit

I'm pretty confused
        myself. I look at
Conner, remember
        the attraction I felt
the first time I saw
        him. Where did that

come from, if I'm
        not gay, or at least
bi? I did ask Dr. Starr
        once if molestation
could cause homosexual
        feelings later in life.

                        Some studies suggest
                                a certain correlation,
                        she said, *but there is no*
                                scientific proof to
                        support that. Truth is,
                                we really don't know

exactly what influences
       sexual preference.
Environment? Genetics?
       Perhaps a combination
of the two? Does it
       really even matter?

Only when you're as
       messed up as me,
I guess. Meanwhile,
       both Conner and
Vanessa are staring,
       waiting for an answer.

"Do I need a label? I
       told you once I've
never had the chance
       to be with a girl, so
how will I know for sure
       until I get that chance?"

I Don't Know What I Am

But suddenly, certainly,
   I want the chance to find
out. And suddenly, certainly,
   I need to know, "Do I
need a label, Vanessa?
    Is it important to you?"

     She moves even closer,
       so close, we're attached.
     If it were, would I be
       here, next to you? I love
     you for the person I've
       discovered under your skin.

I don't feel cold anymore.
    Not outside, not
inside. That space,
   frozen and dead for as
long as I can remember,
    has thawed, come alive.

Another part of me comes
         alive, and it strikes me
that I might not know
         what to do with it, if
Vanessa—or any girl—
         offers me the chance.

I've never "given," only
         been forced to "take."
I've never had sex,
         gift-wrapped with love.
"What's it like?" I ask.
         "Making love to someone?"

                    Vanessa takes my hand.
                         I thought I knew, once
                    or twice before, but now
                         I see there was no love
                    at all between us. I won't
                         know until I make love

                    to you.

Vanessa

Did I Just Say That?

With Conner there?
Conner, who not so very
long ago I thought I wanted
to hook up with?
Instead, I find myself
head over heels in love with—
and desperately wanting
to make love to—"no labels" Tony.
My palms break out
in a nervous sweat and I
whisper, "You don't have
a razor blade on you, do you?"

> *You don't mean that,*
> *do you?* Tony almost pleads.
> *Vanessa, you've stopped*
> *the cutting, haven't you?*
> *Please tell me you've stopped.*

"No worries. I was only
kidding." But I realize
that isn't the truth.

For the last three or four
years, I've dealt with every
nervous moment in my
life by slipping away to
a quiet place and opening
my skin. It's been a ritual,
and for some insane reason,
I want to go there now.

> Tony seems to intuit
> my thoughts. *You sure
> you were only kidding?
> Because if you want
> to cut because of me, I'll
> step out of your life so fast!*

"If you do that," I say,
meaning every word to follow,
"I'll never stop cutting,
lithium or no lithium.
Only love can make me quit."

Do I Really Mean That?

Only time will tell,
I suppose. Anyway, who
knows what will happen
between Tony and me?
For now, I'll make myself
satisfied to sit beside him,
believing he really loves me.
I glance over at Conner,
handsome, self-assured
Conner, who tonight looks
like a lost little boy.
"Hey. You okay?"

> He smiles a sad, strange
> smile. *Yeah, I'm fine.*
> *Just thinking about love*
> *and the strange places*
> *you sometimes find it—*
> *or at least think you do.*

> *You mean like with Emily?*
> Tony asks. *Who was she,*
> *anyway? And what happened*
> *between the two of you?*

Conner hesitates, then
launches a lurid tale
of loving his English
teacher and the inevitable
consequences of being
in love with an older woman.

What about you and Dr. B?
queries Tony. *The two of you
looked pretty tight. Was there
any love there, or just lust?*

No love, plenty of lust,
at least as far as I was
concerned. I thought for a while
she might feel the same way.
But nothing sexual happened
between Heather and me.

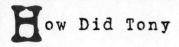ow Did Tony

Pick up on that? I swear,
I never noticed a thing
between Conner and Dr.
Boston—or should I call
her Heather? Holy moley!
I wonder if Conner's attraction
to older women is why
he cooled so completely
toward me. Not much
I could do about that.
Anyway, I don't think
he's "relationship"
material, and I'm really
not in the market for
another one-sided fling.
Still, I'm curious. "So
have you ever fallen
in love with someone
your own age?"

> Conner looks me directly
> in the eye. *One or two,*
> he says. *But I'm poison.*

As the old saying goes,
"sometimes loving someone
means letting them go."

Bullshit! says Tony.
His grip on my hand
tightens, and I sense
impatience in my ever-
patient best friend.
Love means holding on to
someone just as hard as
you can because if you
don't, one blink and
they might disappear

forever.

Conner
What Tony Doesn't Get

Is that love and I are like
water and oil. Put the two
together, blend well, and you
get Quaker State quicksand.

The truth is, I don't have a real
clue what love is—how to
find it, how to give it. Once
upon a time I thought I knew.

But all I really understood
was sex. Sex and love, I've
discovered, are not the same
thing. Life is so complex!

Sex. Love. Athletics. Academics.
My belief in all of those things
is completely shaken. I consider
controlled substance relief,

think better of it. I'm so tired,
I know I'll sleep tonight, wake
up feeling energized, ready to
go ahead, conquer the Challenge,

get out of this place, move ahead
with some sort of a life. Right?
My head is all jumbled. I feel
spent. Dizzy. Nauseous. Numb.

> *Hey, Con*, says Tony. *Do you
> feel okay? Your face is white
> as milk.* His goofy grin does
> not conceal his concern.

Which irritates me somehow.
Guess I'll change the subject.
"So what deep, dark secret did
you not break down and confess?"

Secrets

Yeah, I've still got one or two
that none of the good doctors
managed to pry out. "What's the
worst thing you've ever done?"

> Vanessa's eyes glaze, like
> she's slipped into a trance.
> She considers something,
> shakes her head, tight-lipped.
>
> Finally, she settles on this:
> *I killed someone. I didn't know*
> *him, but I loved him.* She shivers,
> chilled from the inside out.

I don't understand. "How
can you love someone you
don't even know?" And please,
please, Vanessa, tell me who.

> She thinks a minute, then admits,
> *I should have known better*
> *than to get pregnant, but I*
> *thought maybe it would bring*

the father and me closer. When
I told Trevor, he said to get
an abortion. He wouldn't help
pay for it, wouldn't even hold

my hand while I waited to do
that god-awful thing. I went
alone, except for the baby
inside me. It may sound odd,

but I did love that little blob.
Still, I made it die. And when
I think too hard about it, my
insides hurt. Trying not to cry,

Vanessa trembles, and Tony
wraps her with his arms. *Go ahead*
and cry, right here. She lets her
face collapse against his chest.

I Never Expected

Such total, painful honesty.
Can I be as forthright? I've
never told this story to
anyone, not even Dr. B.

"I killed someone too. She
was our au pair, and her name
was Leona. . . ." I know I should
stop there, but somehow I can't.

"I was twelve when she first
came to my bed. She taught me
all I ever needed to know,
fed my hunger for touch,

my need for love. Leona was
my night, my day. I thought
I'd go crazy if she was out
of my sight for more than a few

hours. When I found out she
had another boyfriend—a real,
grown-up boyfriend—I threatened
to tell my mother everything.

Please don't tell, she begged. *I'll*
never find another position.
Like I was going to let her go.
I made up my mind to tell

her boyfriend instead. He caused
an intense scene in our kitchen.
As Leona stormed off, she said,
One day you'll have the sense

to know what you've done. She
sped away, and into a brick wall.
I didn't cry when I heard she
was dead." I'd like to cry now.

Don't know how.

Tony

I've Heard Confession

Is good for the soul.
        Not sure that's so,
but what the hell?
        It might not make me
feel better, but it should
        make Vanessa and Conner

feel better about their
        own guilt trips. "I killed
someone too. But I didn't
        love him. I hated him
with a passion. You were
        twelve when you lost

your virginity? I was eight,
        and I lost it to Larry. I
already told you that,
        and I told you I hurt him
pretty bad. Truth is, I
        killed his sorry ass.

He kept a gun in a lockbox
          inside his car. Dumb
shit never bothered to
          lock the lockbox. I knew
that because a couple
          of times, he pulled out

the gun to threaten my
          ma. One day, after a
particularly bad night
          with Larry, I walked
out to his car, found
          the gun under the seat.

Ma had fixed him
          pancakes for breakfast.
I walked into the kitchen,
          took dead aim at his
Aunt Jemima mouth,
          and pulled the trigger."

The Whole Rotten Truth

Right out in the open.
        And only now it occurs
to me that it might mean
        Vanessa turning her
back on me. I hold her
        even tighter, look into

her eyes, hoping to find
        compassion. "Please tell
me you don't hate me."
        Oh, Tony, she says, *I could*
                never hate you. I understand
        why you did what you did.

                        Okay, everyone, break it
                                up, calls Sean. *We've got*
                        another big day tomorrow.

I wish I could sit here all
        night, holding Vanessa,
kissing her. More.

        But she pulls away. *Guess*
                that's my cue. No worries,
        Tony. I still love you.

"Love you, too." I watch
        her slow retreat, filled
to the brim with loving her.

                Conner taps my shoulder.
                        Hey, Tony. Guess what.
                I don't think you're gay.
It's an amazing concept,
        and so new. "You know,
you just might be right."

We both crawl into our
        sleeping bags, and into
our own little worlds.
        I bet Conner's thinking
about Leona. But there's
        only one person on my mind.

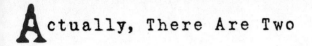

Actually, There Are Two

As everyone else falls
        into Snorezone, I'm
still thinking about
        Vanessa and what she
means to me. As I do,
        Phillip creeps into

my thoughts. "You'd
        like her," I tell him,
very, very quietly,
        so no one hears me
talking to the dead.
        "She's incredible, not

that she's perfect. But you
        once said imperfections
create character. She's got
        character, all right. And,
as you know, I lean way
        toward imperfection myself.

I was really confused
         about this for a while.
Genetics versus learned
         (or forced) behavior
and all. But it sure feels
         real. Sure feels right.

I've never felt so right
         before. Never felt so
in love before. In fact,
         except for you, Phillip,
I can't remember ever
         feeling love for anyone."

         Now an old memory
                  of Phillip floats into
         foggy view. *Tony, I've*
                  never known anyone
         as deserving of love
                  as you. When it finds you,

         don't question it.

Vanessa

I'm Lying Here Shivering

But not because of the weather.
I'm shivering in a frigid indigo
sea. Lithium won't help
this slice of depression.
Thinking about the baby
always drops me here.
It would be a real baby now,
a perfect piece of defective me.

Still, all that was completely
my own fault. I think of Conner,
whose nanny decided to make
him a man. Who knows
what sort of damage
she did to his psyche.

And then there's Tony,
who spent his childhood
locked up because of some
pervert. He should be
a terrible person. Instead,
he's the sweetest, least
selfish guy I've ever known.
How can that be?

And how can it be he's so
in love with me? To grow
up without love, and still
have so much inside?
Just think who he might
have been, had everything
been different for him.
Of course, then I wouldn't
know him now. Love him now.

As everything falls very quiet,
something silent calls to me.
Will the damnable steel
never leave me alone,
never quit whispering
sweet nothings to me?

I Wake, Thankful

I didn't give in to
temptation, hunt for a knife
in the dark of camp, even
though I wanted to so badly.
Will I ever completely
lose the urge to mutilate myself?

> *Everyone up and at 'em,* urges
> Raven. *Are we gonna have
> fun today! Today, we learn
> to climb. You all up for that?*

A chorus of halfhearted
"sures" and "okays" answers
her. But personally, I'm ready.
"Come on, you guys. Rock
climbing is awesome."
Like I have a clue.

> *Not just climbing, but
> spelunking, too. There's an
> outrageous cave not far
> from here. But first, you
> have to master the fine art
> called rappelling.*

Like all art, it takes a certain touch
to do it well. And before
we're through, you will
all do it well. Won't you?

This time she mostly
gets groans for answers.
Only Tony seems almost
as enthusiastic as I am.

He stands, salutes her.
Yes, ma'am, we will all
do it well. He grins in my
direction. *You really want*
to do this, don't you?

I nod. "Don't ask me why.
Maybe a little of my dad
has rubbed off on me, after all."

Raven Guides Us

To the base of a semishort
rock outcropping. First
we go up, then we rappel
down, I assume.

> *First you go up, then*
> *you rappel down. But*
> *the very first thing you*
> *need to learn is how*
> *to belay your climbing*
> *partner. This simple*
> *technique can save a life.*
> *Everyone buddy up.*

For the next two hours,
we learn how about ropes,
carabiners, and ATCs; crotch
loops, leg loops, and slider
buckles. Most important,
we learn about the guide hand,
the brake hand, and how
the two interact. Finally
Raven asks for volunteers.
My (guide) hand shoots up.

Dahlia has little choice but
to go along. *You bitch.*
If I die, I'm coming back
to get you, too. Don't think
I won't be up for it. I'm
half-thinking about it now.

"Fine. You want to be
leader or stay down here?"
She chooses the latter,
and I start to climb, looking
for hand and footholds. It's
not so difficult, and I feel
relatively safe in my harness,
with Dahlia hopefully keeping
the line slack-free and controlled.
"This is easy," I call. And it is.

So far.

Conner

We Spend All Day

Feeding rope to our buddies,
then taking our own turns,
scraping and scrapping up rocks.
Right now, winded and aching,

I'm taking a breather, high
above the blossoming playa.
I swear I can take in a thousand
square miles of view. Too bad

it just looks like a sea of nothing.
I should feel accomplishment.
But all I feel is numb. Numb
and weary, to a surreal degree.

Hey, Conner, calls Tony.
Ready? It's our turn to rappel.

"Coming." Ready or not, I
stand and make myself steady

my trembling legs. I can't
believe how weak I am.

Hey, man, observes my buddy.
You look like you're gonna heave.

I feel like it too, but I can't
admit it. "No worries. I'm fine."

> *You sure? You don't want to be*
> *dangling midair, feeling like shit.*

Anger flashes like lightning.
"I said I'm fucking fine."

> Tony stays cool. *Okay, man.*
> *It's all yours. Go ahead.*

I climb into the harness, fix my
ropes just how Raven showed us.
Then I lower myself over the edge,
thrust myself toward the ground.

It's a Shaky Ride

But I manage it without
puking. One by one, the others
follow, whooping like they're
actually having fun. Jerks.

> Vanessa comes up to me,
> grinning, softly kisses my
> cheek. *Wasn't that amazing?*
> *My head's kind of spinning,*
>
> *but the rest of me feels great.*
> She lays one gentle hand on
> my shoulder, and I notice how
> sunlight plays, gold, on her skin.

Suddenly I want her to
pull me in, hold me close,
absorb me like oxygen.
Suddenly I feel lost. Alone.

What's wrong with me? This girl
is an angel, and I had every
chance to love her. Why must I
rebel against the idea of love?

Now here comes Tony, so in
love with her it's all over
his face. He gives me an easy
shove. *Putting the moves on my girl?*

A green wave of envy washes
over me. Ludicrous! I might
want her, but he deserves her.
"Save it, Ceccarelli. I tried

to steal her from you, but
the best she'd do was give me
a rain check. I strongly
suggest you take good care of her."

Sean interrupts our banter.
*Great job, everyone. Now we'd
better get moving. Surprises
await you all at camp.*

The First Surprise

Is the two-mile walk to reach
our new campsite. We hike
up a narrow canyon, between
two hulking granite walls.

The grade is relatively
steep and I was tired before
we began. No matter how hard
I try, I just can't keep up.

          Tony falls back and walks
          beside me. *Long day, huh?*
His presence persuades
me to lengthen my stride.

"Pretty damn long, all right.
I think I need a vacation."
          He grins. *This* is *your vacation.*
          What I need is a shower. I stink.

He does. We all do. "Water and
soap? What a civilized concept."
          Me? Civilized? He sniffs his armpits.
          Nope. Not even close.

Finally Sean signals us to stop
and make camp. We repeat our
well-practiced routine, then
I tramp out in the brush to piss.

I return to surprise number
two—candy bars, nuts, and beef
jerky, to supplement our roast
turkey, stuffing, and gravy goo.

After dinner, Raven offers
yet a third surprise. *Letters
from home.* She passes them out
like treasure, in the absurd belief

that everyone wants theirs.

Tony

The First Letter

I've ever gotten (except
        for a couple from the state
of Nevada) is from my pa.
        He never even wrote me
when I was in lockup.
        What can he have to say now?

The others withdraw into
        neutral corners. But I need
moral support. I go over
        to Vanessa. "May I sit
next to you? I promise not
        to read over your shoulder."

                She pats the ground beside
                        her. *Of course you can sit
                here. I don't really want
                        to be alone right now either.
                Besides . . . she puffs into
                        the cold air. *You're warm.*

Somehow she doesn't
          notice the smell of
today's exertions.
          Maybe she's olfactory
challenged. Or maybe
          she just doesn't care.

And somehow, her own
          earthy scent turns me
on. I move my leg so it
          touches hers, ankle to
thigh. Her body heat
          turns me on even more.

Completely turned on,
          by a girl. The strangest
thing about feeling this
          way is thinking I've
never *really* been turned
          on before—by anyone.

It's So New

My body telling me
        it really, truly wants
sex. It's so new, knowing
        initiating sex can and
will be up to me. I will
        never be forced to again.

It's so new, this woman
        thing, yet it doesn't feel
foreign. It feels like where
        I've always belonged.
It's so new, equating sex
        with emotion. With love.

Again, I think of Phillip,
        the only person I've ever
felt anything like love for.
        And I'm sure he's smiling.
About Vanessa. About
        my being able to love her.

About the letter in my
        hand. More than once,
he encouraged me to try
        and contact my pa, but
I always refused. *Stubborn*
        as tar, Phillip called me.

> *Are you going to open*
>   *that or what?* Vanessa
> says, rattling the envelope
>   in her own hand. *I'll open*
> *mine if you open yours,*
>   *okay? Ready? One, two . . .*

As we slit the seals, I
        wonder why she has
hesitated this long.
        What secrets of her own
is she still hiding? Will
        she ever share them with me?

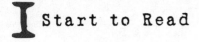Start to Read

Dear Anthony,
        Not long ago you
told me you'd have
        to think about forgiving
me. I hope you have
        found it in your heart

to do so. I won't repeat
        the reasons why I kept
silent for so long. But
        I will reiterate my deep
remorse for not being
        a better father to you.

You may not believe
        this, but I'm proud of
you. After all you've
        been through, you've
risen to every challenge,
        including the ones you're

facing out there in
        the wilderness. I know
you've risen to them,
        because in our few short
times together, I've come
        to see what a truly strong

man you are. Stronger
        than me. Please allow me
the time to get to know
        you. Please allow me
the time to grow to love
        you, and for you to grow

to love me.

Vanessa

I Thought My Letter

Would be from Grandma.
It's not:

Dearest Nessa,

As you know, I'm not much
of a letter writer. But for once
the words seem to be coming
easier, here on paper. When I
saw you at Easter, I couldn't
believe how grown-up you were.
It got me thinking how much
we've lost, with me away all the time.
I wish I could change what has
happened in the past. I can't,
so all that's left is to look to the
future.

I had hoped your mother would
get well one day. But when we visited
her at the hospital, they told me
her catatonia is likely permanent.
She will never come home. So I will.
My request for a Stateside transfer
has been granted. I'll be home
for good once I finish this tour of duty

I also know how much you hated
moving all the time. Don't worry,
We'll stay with my mother, at least
until you go off to college. We can
talk about that later, though.
Right now, I just want you to know
that I will be there for you from now on.

I can't wait to hear about your
experiences, bivouacking
in the Black Rock. Will you show
me around the place,
one day soon?

Love, Daddy

Tony Sighs

Echoing my own feelings.
He reaches for my hand,
and I gratefully slide mine
into the warmth of his.
"You okay?"

> *Yeah, I think so. It's just . . .*
> *kind of confusing.*

"What is?"

> He lifts my hand to his full,
> soft lips. *Everything.*
> *Three months ago*
> *I didn't have a father.*
> *Didn't have you.*
> *Didn't even have a clear*
> *idea of me. All that has*
> *changed, and I'm scared.*

"Why, Tony?"

> *Because before I had*
> *nothing to lose. Now*
> *I've got everything to lose*
> *if I somehow fuck this up.*

"Life is all about change.
If it were static, think
about how boring it would
be. You can't be afraid
of it, and you can't worry
that you'll mess things up.
You deserve good things,
and I want to be one them."

I glance around. Everyone
seems lost in their own
little universe, so I take a big
chance, turning my face
up toward Tony's. My eyes
tell him what I'm too nervous
to say out loud:
Kiss me.

Tony's Kiss

Is like no other kiss, ever.
It wants, but does not demand.
It asks, but doesn't take.
It gives, and pleads for more.
It is filled with desire,
but also curiosity, and it
teaches me that a kiss
should come gift wrapped,
not stripped naked.
Most of all, it makes me
want another kiss
exactly like this one.
It will not be tonight.

*Okay, you two, break
it up*, commands Sean.

Six pairs of eyes have
turned in our direction,
and we are rewarded with
a couple of catcalls.
We slide a little apart,
but not that far.
And now, there is so
much more between us.

Complete connection,
in one innocent kiss.
Okay, maybe not
totally innocent.
Desire stings my body,
in places I've half-
forgotten exist.
But I have to play cool.

Five pairs of eyes
continue to chaperone
us. One pair studies
us, digests what it has
seen, then quickly
returns to the letter,
grasped tightly, tensely,
in muscular hands.

Conner's hands.

Conner

Unbelievable

When I heard we had letters
from home, an insane little part
of me hoped mine might bring
some sliver of affection. Instead:

Conner: Hope all is going
well for you, and that your
time in the outback has kept
you fit. You must excel at your

football tryouts. They expect
you to fail. I'm sure, however,
you'll prove them very wrong.
One small detail, which I'll mention

here: you have some makeup work
to do to keep you on track
for early graduation. If you
pursue it diligently this summer,

you won't have to play catch-up
in the fall. By the way, your father
and I have sent applications
to all the colleges on our list.

All you have to do is maintain
your GPA and, of course, score
well on your entrance exams.
Not really much more to say

except to let you know Cara
has already been accepted
at Stanford. You can do as well.
After all, you're her twin. Mom.

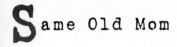

Same Old Mom

Same ugly comparisons
between Cara and me.
Same expectations, and what
did she mean, "on *our* list"?

Sean interrupts my reverie.
Okay, you two, break it up.

He means Vanessa and Tony,
and when I glance their way

I catch the end of a kiss.
Another slap of jealousy
catches me off guard, jerks
my head in the other direction.

My eyes fall to the paper
clutched in my hands. I can't
remember one time my mom's
lips touched a part of my face.

Surely not my own lips—shades
of incest. But neither did she
ever kiss my cheek or even
my forehead. Oh, to be blessed

by a kiss like the one I just
witnessed. I'd trade every kiss
I've stolen for one, given
like that. Who could have guessed

such a thing would happen
between Vanessa and Tony—
two fractured people, healed
(perhaps) by unforeseen,

not to mention unlikely,
love. I'm more than jealous.
I'm downright covetous.
I can't think about it anymore.

Can't think about Cara, Stanford,
football. Can't think about my
parents, grades, test scores. Can't
think about any of that at all.

I Fold the Letter

Into a perfect paper
airplane, take a walk under
sequined night sky, try to
silence the chatter in my brain.

The sound of cheerful voices
drifts toward me from camp.
Their letters are tucked into
pockets and sleeping bags, gifts.

Rewards for accomplishments
and, with any luck at all, change.
But nothing has changed for me.
I'll go home to the same grand

house in the same manicured
neighborhood. (Except for the new
neighbors at the end of the block.
Exorcism, "for my own good.")

I'll go home to expectations
no way I can live up to, no
longer want to. But I've never
had a say about my future.

I close my eyes, and all
I can see is my mother's
face. Sculpted. Beautiful.
Angry. So often angry.

And I am so much like her.
A grenade of my own anger
explodes inside my head.
I am damaged. Decayed.

A gust of wind roughs up
my hair. The paper airplane
sits heavy in my hand. I cock
back my arm, release, let it fly

straight to hell.

Tony

I Swim Up into Morning

And thoughts of Vanessa,
          reaching up to kiss me.
I sit up, look for her,
          but she's nowhere in
sight, and a strange
          jolt of worry strikes.

"Come on, Tony," I tell
          myself. "She's just off
for her morning . . ."
          Finishing the thought
seems voyeuristic.
          What's up with me?

                    Hey, you. Vanessa's voice
                              sneaks over my shoulder,
                    settles softly in my ear.
                              Did you know you snore?
                    She moves around in front
                              of me, eyes lifting to mine.

"Me? Snore? You must
          have me confused with
someone else!" I answer
          the shake of her head
with a smile. "Well, why
          were you listening, anyway?"

> *I couldn't sleep. I kept*
> *   thinking about this guy*
> *and how good a kisser*
> *   he was and how much*
> *I wanted to kiss him again.*
> *   Even if he did snore.*

God, I love her. She is
          just the most incredible
person I've ever known.
          Funny. Smart. Pretty.
One day, very soon, I want
          to do more than kiss her.

But Right Now

Everyone's staring, like
   they're reading my mind
or something. I excuse
   myself for my own a.m.
stroll. I return to gossip
   and breakfast, in that order.

   Lori's mom and dad are
      getting back together,
   Dahlia informs us all.

      It was my fault they broke
         up in the first place, Lori
      explains. *No pressure there!*

      Justin launches a sermon.
         Just give it to the Lord.
      He'll see you through.

Hey, Raven, calls Dahlia.
      Any candy bars left? I love
chocolate for breakfast!

Blah, blah, blah. Only
          Conner is quiet. Sulky.
Pissed, even. The look on
          his face is hard to decipher.
But I'm guessing his letter
          was less than inspirational.

"Hey, Conner," I call.
          "Don't tell me my
snoring kept you awake
          too!" I expect a grin.
A finger. Something.
          But he just sits there.

Half of me wants
          to go over and hug
him. The other half
          wants to shake him.
Both halves agree he
          wants to be left alone.

Both Halves Decide

To leave Conner alone.
　　　Anyway, it's time
to start off the day
　　　with a delicious MRE
and a cup of black coffee.
　　　The breakfast of warriors.

　　　　　　　Okay, listen up, Raven
　　　　　　　　　barks. *You all did a
　　　　　　　fantastic job yesterday.
　　　　　　　　　I think you've all got
　　　　　　　the hang of climbing,
　　　　　　　　　so to speak. Tomorrow*

　　　　　　　*we'll explore the cave
　　　　　　　　　I told you about. You'll
　　　　　　　have to rappel a long way
　　　　　　　　　down into a very dark
　　　　　　　cavern. Then you'll have
　　　　　　　　　to climb back up out.*

　　　　　　　*Before we can trust
　　　　　　　　　you to do that, we
　　　　　　　want to test your skills.*

Today we'll practice
on some very tall, very
        steep granite walls.

It is imperative that
        you double-check your
equipment and knots
        before you begin your
ascent. I'll take lead
        today. Sean will hang

out below. Be sure
        to have him inspect
your ropes before you
        start to climb. We don't
want to have to scrape
        what's left of you off

the rocks.

Vanessa
Watching Raven

Climb gives me the chills.
She works and works for holds
in the megalithic wall, fixes
protection at strategic points
along the way. Up. Up. Up.
Makes me dizzy, just looking
up that high. So why
am I so excited, knowing
my turn is coming?

> *If you smile any wider,*
> *you're going to crack*
> *your face right in half.*
> Tony drapes an arm
> around my shoulder.
> *You really like this stuff,*
> *don't you?*

"Yeah. And it definitely
surprises me. I've never
been much of a thrill seeker . . ."
Except in my manic phases.
And the thrills I sought
were nothing like this.

". . . I like to ski—wide, groomed
runs. Not trees. Not bumps.
I like to mountain bike—ride
a chair lift up, coast down.
I'm not an athlete. Not
even close. This is really
hard. But I love it."

I just hope it isn't mania
talking. But it doesn't feel
that way. In fact, for the first
time in a very long time,
I feel completely grounded.
Except, of course,
when I'm climbing.

Since Sean's Going Last

He buddies Tony with Justin.
Tony takes lead, and I watch
him climb, confident and strong.
Funny, I never noticed
how fit he was until the Challenge.
He never complains,
never makes excuses.
He just accomplishes.

Sean calls, *Come on, Vanessa.*
You and Dahlia go next.
Let's go over your
equipment. He tests
my harness, helmet, ropes.
Hold on a minute. Check
this out. See how you've
got your rope over the gate
of the carabiner? That's
called back clipping. Put
any stress at all on the 'biner,
it's liable to pop open
and let the rope slide out.
Could be ugly.

With everything adjusted
correctly, it's my turn
to climb. "Do you want
lead?" I ask Dahlia.

> You crazy, man? Lead is
> dangerous, and this wall
> is insane. You go first.
> If you can make it, so can I.

I follow Raven's route,
clipping onto the anchors
she has already placed
in the rocks. Looking up,
I see Tony, measuring my
every move, nodding to let
me know I'm looking good.

And feeling great.

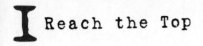 Reach the Top

Swing a leg over, and here
I am, thousands of feet
above the playa floor.
I can see forever up here,
and it makes me feel
just about invincible.

> Tony runs over, picks
> me up, swings me in circles.
> *Isn't this awesome? No*
> *wonder you like this sport.*
> *We'll have to do it again*
> *once we're out of here.*
> He slows, puts me down.
> Gets very serious.
> *I will still see you once*
> *we're out of here, won't I?*

Everything has been day-
to-day, and I haven't really,
truly thought about what
it will be like once we put
Aspen Springs behind us.

But one thing's for sure.
"Of course you'll see me.
Maybe even more
of me than you'll want to.
I'm the tiniest bit obsessive
about the people I love."

> *Good. We're on the same*
> *page. I don't really know*
> *where I'll go or what I'll*
> *do when I'm "free."*
> *All I know is my life would*
> *be empty without you in it.*

I look into his eyes, and what
I find there fills me with hope.
He knows all my secrets,
even the worst of them.
Despite everything, he still

loves me.

Conner

God, I'm Tired

I can barely pull myself
to my feet, let alone up
a hundred-foot rock wall. Sleep—
deep sleep—would be so sweet.

> I'm the last to go, and Sean
> wants me to take lead. *You*
> *can do it. Just clip onto*
> *the anchors before you pull*
>
> *yourself up. If those petite*
> *girls can handle it, you can*
> *handle it better. It's all up*
> *to you, man. Get climbin'.*

I stand at the bottom, looking
up at where the others wait.
I feel like the idiot kid
who can't say no to a dare.

Fuck it. What do I have to
lose? The first anchor is
maybe eight feet up. I study
the rock face, choose the best

way to reach the anchor, clip
on, and pull. My fingers ache
and I think my knuckles will
swell later. This is bullshit.

But then, my entire life
is bullshit. The best things
in it have vanished, ghosts.
Ghosts I'll admit I created.

The rope holding me in place
creaks, stressed by my weight.
                    Keep going, buddy, yells Sean.
                    You can rest when you get to the top.

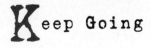eep Going

That's exactly what I tell
myself. "Keep going, loser."
I'll never be anything else.
I step on a narrow rock shelf

and it crumbles, making
me scramble for a foothold.
I find one, push up, smash my
knee into a jut of granite.

Way to go, faggot. The voice
I hear belongs to my father.
*Get hold of yourself. You'll never
make first string like that.* Fear

of failure impels me toward
the top, as it pushed me toward
the goal line so many times
before. I don't dare stop.

Don't dare drop the ball. Don't
dare finish second. *We only
want what's best for you, so
spare me your whining. Why*

*can't you be like Cara? She
never loses.* Cara is smarter.
Cuter. More talented. I will
forever ride in her backseat.

Well, they're fraternal *twins, you
see.* Now the voice is my mom's.
I want to shut her up, but I
know she won't be silenced.

I reach up for a handhold,
find I'm almost to the top.
And still the home movies
rewind . . . replay . . . rewind.

*Of course I'm proud of Conner.
It's just . . . he's not his sister.*
With a burst of energy, I
thrust myself up and over.

Standing Here

My entire world far beneath
my feet, I should be filled
with pride. Instead, I feel
overwhelmed by a sense of defeat.

Suddenly it comes to me,
toes tempted to test the ledge,
that there is a way out of this.
Calm surety flows through

my veins, and as I turn to wave
good-bye, I wonder if it will
hurt or if a single person
will cry at my funeral.

I take a deep breath, a final
taste of sweet mountain air.
I conjure Leona, Emily.
Move my feet closer. Closer.

There's Grandma One, Grandma
Two, and their spouses, waiting
for me. I see Dad. Cara. Mommy.
I screw up my courage, step over . . .

Tony

Raven Screams

Conner, no! Mary,
> *holy mother of God.*
And then she runs.

Conner? What happened
> to Conner? We follow
Raven to the cliff's edge.
> One glance over the side
tells a simple story,
> one I refuse to believe.

"Quick! Someone belay
> me. I'll go get him. Call
911. Maybe there's still
> time to save him. Will
somebody please help me?
> I've got to get down to him!"

> Raven just stands, two-way
> > in hand. *Sean's almost*
> *up to him. But no one,*
> > *no one could survive*
> *that fall.* Within seconds,
> > her radio spits the expected news.

Guilt balloons inside me,
        shoves me to my knees.
"Oh God, no. It's not true!"

                Gentle arms tuck me in.
                        Stop, Tony. He's gone.
                Vanessa's tear-dampened
                        kisses cover my face.
                *Oh! I can't believe he'd
                        do such a horrible thing.*

"I can. And I could have
        prevented it. It's all my
fault, Vanessa. I knew."
        I push her away, turn
my head to one side.
        My vomit tastes like death.

Raven Calls for Rescue

Care Flight isn't far
        away, at least not as
the crow (or 'copter) flies.
        But rather than wait,
we opt to climb down.
        We have to go past Conner.

Part of me doesn't want
        to look. Most of me has
to. He's splayed on a big
        boulder. His spirit, or
whatever was inside,
        is definitely somewhere

else. All that's left is his
        broken shell. His eyes
are open, as if he couldn't
        let go of the very last
thing he saw. I wonder
        what it was. Heaven?

He's smiling, and one
         hand is extended. Did
someone come for him,
         take his hand, and walk him
across that border, into
         the ultimate frontier?

Some churches say
         suicide denies him
that comfort. But could
         a true and loving God
turn His back on such
         a tortured soul? Wouldn't

the Ultimate Tribunal
         consider extenuating
circumstances? Will
         it consider them for me?
"Please, Father. Please,
         Conner. Forgive me."

The "Rescue"

Isn't much of a rescue,
　　　　of course. They can
take their time, and
　　　　they do. We gather
at the base of the hill,
　　　　watch the crew's efforts.

Another time, another
　　　　body, it might be
interesting, how they
　　　　lower a sled from the top,
gentle the remains into
　　　　a polyurethane bag, zip. . . .

But those remains belong
　　　　to my friend. I haven't
had many of those. Now
　　　　this one is gone. Forever.
I should cry, want to cry.
　　　　All I can do is feel ice cold.

Vanessa and I huddle
         together, searching
for comfort in each
         other's touch. "Why
couldn't he just talk
         to me, Vanessa?"

                    He did talk to you, Tony.
                              I think you were the only
                    person he could talk to
                              at all. In the long run,
                    maybe that wasn't enough.
                              But this wasn't your fault.

"I knew he'd quit taking
         his meds, knew how
depressed he seemed.
         I never said a word.
And that will haunt
         me for the rest of my life."

Maybe even longer.

Vanessa
Care Flight Lifts Off

And in its wake, seven
people seem unable to move,
stunned into silent shock.

> Finally Sean decides,
> *Let's go back to camp.*
> *Aspen Springs will send*
> *transport, but it will take*
> *a while to get here.*

.

We walk slowly, trying
to absorb what has happened.
Everyone deals with the loss
in different, personalized ways.

> Sean and Raven discuss
> the possible fallout. *I knew*
> *he was struggling,* Sean
> says. *But when I talked*
> *to him, he seemed okay.*
> *He said he was just tired.*
> *Did I push him too hard?*

Damn, what a waste!
Dahlia tells Lori, who agrees,
That boy was fine.
Justin just prays.

Tony holds on to my hand
like if he let go, I might dash
over a cliff too. I know he needs
me more than ever. The responsibility
is daunting, and I think about
a kiss from my steel lover,
knowing I have to find a way
to leave it far behind me.

*Do you think Conner's parents
know yet?* asks Tony.

"I'm sure they must."

Do you think they care?

The Question

Takes me by surprise.
"Of course they care."
They have to, don't they?
"Why would you ask
such a question?"

> *I was just thinking*
> *about who would care*
> *if I killed myself. I never*
> *thought about anyone else*
> *when I tried before.*
> *Of course, I didn't really*
> *have anyone to think*
> *about then. Ma was gone,*
> *not that she would have*
> *given a fraction of a damn.*
> *Phillip was gone, and Pa*
> *was just a memory.*
> He stops walking, pulls
> me tight against his chest.
> *And I didn't know you.*
> *Would you care, really care?*

I reach my arms up around
his neck, pull his face down,
lock his eyes with mine.
"Yes, Tony. I would really care.
Losing you would kill
a part of me—the part
that has learned what
love really is."

And what is that?

"You." This time
when we kiss, I feel
it in the pit of my stomach,
I feel it in my heart.
And I realize love isn't about sex.
It's about connection.

Camp Feels Empty

While we wait for transportation
to carry us out of this place,
Tony and I take a walk.
It's a perfect spring day
on a hill above the Black Rock
Desert. "This was an island
once, you know, when the playa
was underwater. Can you believe
all that desert was once a giant lake?"

> Tony stares out at the ocean
> of sage and bitterbrush.
> *It is hard to believe*
> *that something that seems*
> *so permanent was once*
> *so different. Change.*
> *I guess that really is one*
> *thing you can count on. . . .*
>
> He is quiet for several
> minutes. Finally he says,
> *I just can't figure out why.*

I mean, I can understand
why someone like me
would think suicide was
the only way out. But
Conner had it all—he
was great looking,
smart, rich. He had
everything to live for.
So, why . . .

A breeze blows up,
touching my cheek
like a little child's kiss.
It flutters a piece of paper,
lodged in the sage.
"Trash, out here? Must
belong to one of us."

We move closer,
and when I reach
for it, I find . . .

. . . a perfect paper airplane.